PRISONER'S DILEMMA

Vish Dhamija is the bestselling author of ten works of crime fiction, including *Unlawful Justice*, *Bhendi Bazaar*, *The Mogul*, *The Heist Artist* and *Doosra*. He is frequently referred to in the Indian press as the 'master of crime and courtroom drama'. In August 2015, after the release of his first legal thriller, *Déjà Karma*, *Glimpse* magazine called him 'India's John Grisham' for stimulating the genre of legal fiction in India. Vish lives in London with his wife, Nidhi.

ALSO BY VISH DHAMIJA

Nothing Lasts Forever
Bhendi Bazaar
Déjà Karma
Doosra
Nothing Else Matters
Unlawful Justice
The Mogul
The Heist Artist
Lipstick

PRISONER'S DILEMMA

VISH
DHAMIJA

PAN

First published 2021 by Pan
an imprint of Pan Macmillan Publishing India Private Limited
707, Kailash Building
26 K. G. Marg, New Delhi 110 001
www.panmacmillan.co.in

Pan Macmillan, 6 Briset St, Farringdon, London EC1M 5NR
Associated companies throughout the world
www.panmacmillan.com

ISBN 978-93-89109-77-1

Typeset in Minion Pro by R. Ajith Kumar, New Delhi
Printed and bound in India by
Replika Press Pvt. Ltd.

For Theodora Asimakou
(1971–2020)
The memory remains, Dora!

AUTHOR'S NOTE

PRISONER'S DILEMMA IS AN ASPECT OF GAME THEORY that shows why two rational individuals might not or cannot cooperate with each other, even if it is in their best interest to do so. The best example of it was narrated to me by one of my business school professors.

Two final-year male college students went out drinking on the eve of their economics examination. They met some girls, one thing led to another and all of them ended up drunk. When they woke up in the morning, they realized they had missed their examination. The two concocted a story – they told the professor that one of them had an ailing mother they had to go out of town to meet and, on the way back, their car had a flat tyre, and hence they couldn't get back in time. The two were good students, so the professor empathized with them, but he insisted he couldn't give them the same questions he'd given the others since those questions had already been revealed, making it unfair for the rest of the class. Instead, he asked them to return the following day so he could prepare a fresh set of questions for them.

When the two turned up to take their test the next day, they were made to sit in separate rooms, and the professor gave them a paper with a single question: *Which tyre?*

DAY ONE

———

THURSDAY, 16 JANUARY 1997
SADAR POLICE STATION
GURGAON, HARYANA

1

JAILBIRDS

'WHY AM I HERE?' BIPIN DESAI ASKED.

But his voice quivered. A film of nervous sweat covered his forehead. Thank god for the eyebrows that stopped the sweat from getting into his eyes. He had never perspired so much before, but this place was boiling. The small eight-by-eight room made him feel claustrophobic – or was it the ominous thoughts of what lay in store that were making him sweat like a pig? It must take some effort to make a room so hot in the peak of winter in Delhi, he thought to himself. Had they placed burning coal on the roof just to agonize him? Or somehow pumped imperceptible warm gas into the room? Was it retribution of some kind? It was possible that he was feeling the heat since he was anxious, frightened and confused in equal parts. He knew *why* he was where he was; what startled him was *how* he had ended up there and, more importantly, how it had all unravelled so soon.

The policeman sat motionless in front of him, seemingly lost in his thoughts. He had stumbled into the room, as though tripping on an invisible wire, but broke his fall by placing his hands on the table. The file in his hands landed atop the table, a few papers slithering out, which he reassembled meticulously until every sheet of paper and all the edges matched evenly – like his life depended on it. Bipin wondered if this man also counted his steps while walking. Maybe he suffered from obsessive compulsive disorder to some degree.

The inspector hadn't uttered a word since entering the room about five minutes ago, which was almost an hour since Bipin had been locked here. In the name of refreshments, they had provided a glass of water, which wasn't even cold. No tea or coffee was offered. He wished he could get his hands on a chilled bottle of cola just to beat the suffocating heat in the room, but the stingy bastards in the constabulary had given him nothing. And this was when Haryana was one of the affluent states in India, and Gurgaon its nucleus of commerce.

'Why am I here?'

Still no response. It was like the inspector hadn't heard him.

'What's the charge against me?' Bipin asked again. He glanced at the file the inspector had brought in and was lying on the rusty steel table bolted to the floor. The three-by-two table sat between Bipin and the police officer. It was a small interrogation room, where the police brought suspects who were chargesheeted, but not yet convicted. Unlike in Bollywood films, the questioning didn't take place in some windowless basement where the accused was stripped, suspended upside down and beaten black and blue until they provided all the information sought by the police. And although this was not one of those state-of-the-art interrogation rooms one saw on American television, where one side of the room had a one-way glass for the other members of the police team to observe, this room had a camera with a microphone. Anything that took place here – conversation, action, the accused's expressions, mannerisms, deflections – would be recorded. These would be analysed and re-analysed later; the recording might be presented in court subsequently if the person confessed to the crime or gave up his co-conspirators. The camera would also ensure, given the unfortunate reality of policing in our country, that no policeman – irrespective of rank and position – ever took the law into their own hands. If the police weren't policed, they'd become the biggest organized gang, wouldn't they?

'I'm Arfy Khan, Senior Inspector, Haryana Police. What's your name, sonny boy?' the police officer asked, breaking Bipin's brief reverie, with one of his eyebrows raised like a comedian in some B-grade Hindi film.

'It's written on top of the file you just carried in, so what's the point of asking me?' Bipin said.

'Bipin Desai, oh, yes!' The inspector pretended like he hadn't thought of that. He opened the file and read

monotonously: 'Son of Mr Harish Desai, resident of New
Delhi, age twenty-six ...' Bipin Desai was short, squat and
prematurely balding. He was around sixty-five kilos on
a five-feet-six frame. He wore rimless glasses and had a
college degree. There was nothing conspicuous about him
– a fairly average guy next door, whom someone could see
and forget in the same instant – a bald and spectacled guy.
Nothing more.

'Yes.'

'Thanks for confirming.'

'What am I doing here?' Bipin repeated.

'Are you a broken gramophone record or do you think
I'm stone deaf or brain-dead that I didn't hear you the first
couple of times?' Arfy Khan snapped.

*Who was he? Some clown they had sent in to talk to
him?* 'But you did not respond,' he said softly, keeping his
temper in check.

'That's because I'm ignoring your ridiculous question,
since *I* know that *you* know why you're here,' Arfy sounded
like he was stating the obvious.

Bipin stared at him unflinchingly. If he was to maintain
that he was innocent, the facade was essential.

'Besides, the way things work in this room is I get to
ask all the questions, and you respond to them. Not the
other way around. If you act like a good boy, I'll give you
some answers. You show good behaviour, you will earn
brownie points.' Arfy said dispassionately. He didn't change
his tone, but there was something in the way he spoke

and in his demeanour that would have brought instant laughter to most. Even hardened criminals facing long sentences and a grim future would find him funny. He was unlike the police officers that brought out the fear of God in most criminals. Maybe it was his personality. There wasn't anything inherently funny about him – except for his fall into the room to start with; he was actually quite a handsome man: about five-feet-ten, clean shaven, with thick bushy eyebrows, high cheekbones and a sharp nose. He had a short police haircut, and the khaki uniform sat on his skin like the colour was developed exclusively to suit his olive complexion. He was dapper even in uniform. Compared to the policemen Bipin had seen in real life or on reel, Senior Inspector Arfy Khan looked the complete opposite. No potbelly with shirt buttons stretching over it, no *paan* in the mouth, no crass language. He must be thirty or thereabouts, Bipin reckoned. A charmer, not a menacer – the proverbial good cop in the good-cop-bad-cop routine, which meant there was a bad cop lurking somewhere in the vicinity, waiting on the sidelines to enter the picture.

A fresh chill ran down Bipin's spine. He looked around the room. Having spotted the camera as soon as he was brought in, he knew he was being watched. If he uttered anything it would be heard and recorded, so he had kept his mouth shut. He didn't look conspicuously at it either. But now, when the apparently amiable policeman sat there asking him questions, the thought of the camera – and being watched – once again took over his thoughts. He nodded in response.

'Did you understand what I just said?' asked the inspector. Still friendly, still cordial, still smiling.

'Yes, sir.'

'So do you want to tell me where the cash is?'

'The what …?'

'Sonny boy, if you really want to sit here and play games, I can ask someone to bring in Snakes and Ladders, and we can play that. Or Ludo if you prefer.'

Bipin said nothing. He had heard or read somewhere that the less one spoke in the presence of the police, the better. You inadvertently ended up giving something away. Why risk it?

Accepting the silence as his response, Arfy scoffed and stood up. He held the table edges like he'd slip if he didn't. 'I'll be back in a while. Why don't you take this time and think and work on your responses? If you are going to lie, at least try to be original.'

'Could I get something to drink, please? Something cold?'

'Do you want a chilled Kingfisher?' He was polite but noticeably sarcastic.

'No, just a soft drink would do, please?'

'I apologize for bringing you to a police station. If I had known you wanted a cold drink, I'd have taken you to some bar or restaurant. We could have had a drink, watched some TV, listened to music and had a jolly time, but over here I'll see what I can do,' he said and walked out. Bipin heard Arfy fumble with the key on the other side of the door for a few minutes before he managed to secure the lock on the outside. Then he heard the inspector's footsteps fade into the distance.

2

FREE BIRDS

HOW COULD SUCH A WELL-DEVISED PLAN GO SO HORRIBLY wrong? And in a matter of days. How? They had planned for weeks and months, taken every possible precaution, worn gloves, used disguises, been secretive to the extent of worrying their work colleagues because the others found them a little self-absorbed, even distanced themselves from their families. How then? Maybe there had been some misunderstanding. Bipin was paranoid and maybe – just maybe – all wasn't lost and things weren't as sinister as he was imagining them to be. Time to put Plan B into action.

But they never had a Plan B.

Shit! Shit! Shit!

Where was Anuj? For a moment he felt a little light-headed. Thank god they hadn't been together. If Anuj was safe, the loot was safe. Over a crore. Once Anuj figured out that his friend had been arrested, he'd hire the best lawyer and get him out of here. He'd post the bail ASAP.

At least, money was one thing they didn't have to worry about anymore. Wasn't that the whole point of being rich?

They had been friends since primary school: Bipin Desai and Anuj Shastri. Having spent their innocent years together in Munirka, an urban locality in southwest Delhi, both the boys came from similar backgrounds – their fathers were in government service and their mothers, homemakers. Anuj was physically bigger and stronger and better-looking. He was also the more adventurous of the two. Tall – about six feet now – he had long hair and no glasses, fine bone structure, sharp features, bright eyes and a smiling face. He could walk in and light up a room instantly. Most girls gave him a second or third look. To top it all, he was extremely charming. But what Bipin lacked in the physical department, he more than made up for in the mental faculty. He was certainly the brighter of the two. He was the one who got better grades, the one who planned everything, and had been instrumental in planning the heist. Anuj couldn't have conceptualized it or executed it if it were not for him. He was a bit thick cerebrally and also a bit short-tempered. Passionate, bordering on rash.

In college, the two friends had met another like-minded soul from a similar background – Manasi Upadhaya. She had recently moved to Delhi from somewhere in Gujarat, where her father had worked at the Life Insurance Corporation of India. Considering their financial backgrounds, the three families resided in

apartments built by the Delhi Development Authority –
DDA flats, as they were called – and had always lived a
simple, middle-class life. They lacked nothing when it
came to education or clothes – their parents provided
everything they could, and everything had been perfect
until school. Most fellow students wore uniforms; there
wasn't much to flash around, but college life had opened
their eyes. While at Dyal Singh College on Lodhi Road,
when the three became thick friends in the second year,
it became evident to the trio that they were kind of
underclass, underprivileged kids unlike some others who
drove cars to college, wore expensive, branded clothes
and socialized amongst themselves. There was a huge
class divide. And although the rich kids weren't rude or
condescending in any way – hellos were always exchanged –
it was obvious that they did not want to mix with the likes
of Manasi, Anuj and Bipin. Maybe the rich ones thought
that the middle-class students would dirty their pool, or
that there wasn't much in common to socialize with their
poor classmates; maybe they thought that their parents
might disapprove of their association with the have-nots;
or maybe it just never occurred to them to include those
who were not in their league. They were blissfully unaware
of how fortunate they were and the kind of envy they
evoked in those less fortunate. Whatever the case might
have been, the reality stung. Initially, it was individual,
but as the bond between the three grew stronger, they
discovered that those feelings were shared. It would

have been good to be rich, but not much could be done. The parents of all three had worked hard to provide a roof, clothing and college education. What else could be expected of them? If anything, it was in the hands of their children to change their fates.

'I'll never work at a nine-to-five government job,' Anuj declared.

'Me neither,' Manasi seconded.

'Why, what's wrong with it? It provides stability in life, pays enough to get food on the table, get married, send kids to school. I mean I know I would want a Maruti Esteem too right away, but we shouldn't forget we are a million times better off than a lot of kids who never go to school or have to work at minimum wages to barely survive.'

'Once a middle-class, always a middle-class,' Manasi jested.

'Do you have a better idea?'

'I'd rather prostitute myself than work for the government and earn peanuts.'

'Well, at least you have the looks and the body for it,' retorted Bipin, clearly not happy with her line of thought.

Manasi wasn't in the same league as a film actress, but she was attractive. Petite with shoulder-length, straight, espresso-coloured hair, she had big, beautiful eyes. At five-feet three, she was always impeccably dressed and well-groomed and a lot of boys from their own side of the tracks ogled her. But she was always bothered that she was

somehow invisible to all the rich ones, even though she
was a lot better-looking than the girls the rich boys fancied
and drove around with. It hurt.

———

Everyone started college on a high – the hopes and dreams
of education, a well-paying job at the end of the degree, but
for most it had an unexpected and unpleasant end. It was
a call to wake up and face the harsh reality: the promised
rainbow wasn't within reach for the middle classes, not
even in sight. The number of jobs available didn't match
the number of people graduating every year. Competition
was tough. For Manasi, Anuj and Bipin, the prospect
wasn't any brighter. Their aspirations started fading after
the final year when every job they applied for had more
than a few hundred applicants. Three months after the
graduation results, even a clerical job in a government
office seemed attractive. But even the Government of India
wasn't knocking on doors in the DDA flats in Munirka
looking for three graduates from Dyal Singh College.
There was far fiercer competition for public-sector jobs
because despite the low salaries they provided stable,
pensionable employment.

Mr Upadhaya was convinced his precious daughter was
meant to be an IAS or IPS officer – the best public-sector
job out there. No question about it. Or else they would
start looking for a suitable groom for Manasi, get her

married into another bourgeois family where the groom was employed at a secure government job, preferably in a senior-officer position. After all, his daughter was fair and beautiful; who wouldn't want her as their wife or daughter-in-law? Mrs Upadhaya had little say in her husband's decision. Her father had exercised the same right, using the same rationale, to get her married to Manasi's father, hadn't he? And what was wrong with that? She had been happy, her husband had provided for her, she had raised two beautiful daughters, and life – despite the financial ups and downs – hadn't treated her too badly. Some of her friends had done far worse. So what if they still didn't have a Maruti? Overall, marriage had worked out for her, as it had for her elder daughter, Manjula, who was happily married to a class-III gazetted officer in Bhilwara, Rajasthan, a transferable job with good perks, and splendid prospects of promotions; they even had a son now. Things would work out for Manasi too.

However, the idea of getting married at such a young age was not as appealing to Manasi as it had been for her sister. Manjula had married a man eight years older. Manasi, on the other hand, was only twenty-one and had no intentions of letting a thirty-year-old man she didn't know marry her for her youth. She wasn't going to spread her legs for someone who didn't value her beyond her pretty face and fit body. The alternative was to yield to her father's advice, be an obedient daughter and start preparing for the Indian Administrative Services entrance exams. She had got decent grades in college, but so had many of her classmates; however, unlike her father, she didn't think she had the ability to study sixteen to eighteen hours a day, like others who prepared for the IAS entrance exam did. Barring a massive stroke of luck, even if she cleared the preliminary tests – the odds of her winning the lottery were better. But she decided it was a good way to avoid delivering babies right away – her sister was already pregnant with child number two. She could, under the pretext of studying for entrance exams, look for other, more preferable prospects. And if she found a half-decent job in the private sector which her father abhorred – *It's not something that girls from decent families do. You will become a secretary at best ... Hare Krishna.'* – as he had told her more than once. His upbringing in the fifties, and his job with the LIC had never exposed him to the opening of the private sector where women were competing with men in all industries. *'It's the nineties,'* she had wanted to yell back, but the debate would have been pointless. You couldn't straighten a dog's tail no matter how much you tried. Hers, like so many other middle-class families where only the male members worked, was deeply rooted in patriarchy. The husband or the father had the final say in all matters of concern. But if she got a well-paying job, she'd fight the battle that day. Until then, she went back to studying and attending coaching classes like a dutiful daughter.

3

FREE BIRDS

ANUJ SHASTRI HAD HAD A ROUGH TIME AFTER GRADUATING from college. Manasi had started studying for competitive exams, and she didn't have as much free time to meet as during their college days. Anuj liked her. No, he loved her. But with no job, and not even a remote prospect of one, it seemed pointless to confess his feelings to her. What would he propose in any case? Come, and we could waste time together? Moreover, he had an inkling that Bipin loved her too. The three had started out as mere friends, but as inevitably happens between young men and women, a physical attraction had developed, and with that came feelings of love, of belonging. Neither of the two boys had confessed their feelings to her, but if either of them did, they knew she would reciprocate or it would destroy the relationship forever; not just with her, but between all three of them, probably. The fear of losing a friend kept them restrained for the time being.

And Manasi wasn't the only one who was busy. Bipin was occupied too: he had found a job in the retail sector. He became financially independent to some extent, while Anuj still lived with his parents. His father had started citing his son's friends as successes.

They have some aim in life, unlike you.

They're progressing in their careers, unlike you.

The 'unlike you' was figured in every taunt, in every sarcastic comment.

Bipin, a wimp, working for a greengrocer after graduating in science, and Manasi – it made him chuckle – appearing for IAS exams. Seriously? What had happened to all their philosophical discussions in college about dreaming big? Anuj knew that there was no way Manasi could clear the IAS examinations. In a few years, after the three sanctioned attempts, her ambitious plan would end and her father would get her married. And Bipin – what were the long-term career prospects from a job in a grocery shop? Was he going to work for a baker next?

He loved both of them but it was excruciating for him to listen to his father go on and on about his friends being more successful than him. Sometimes it was so unbearable he wanted to yell back, but instead he would go and spend a few days with Bipin who had rented a small one-bedroom studio in Noida. His mother was the only reason he returned home every time. His relationship with his father had been dysfunctional for as long as he could recall.

Have you done your homework, boy? Look at your marks in maths; you need to work hard, boy. Oye ladke, don't spend too much time watching television. Run and get me a glass of water, boy.

Boy? The man couldn't even care enough to address him as *son*?

But lately, his father's remarks had grown harsher. Anuj was an only child, and his father was about to retire. A senior clerk at a nationalized bank, Mr Shastri could not continue supporting Anuj on his retirement pension. Consequently, he wanted his son to start earning and take responsibility of the family. If not, at the very least, get a decent job like his friend, so that he would no longer drain their resources after his retirement, which was merely two years away. The earlier Anuj left home, the sooner they could start saving some money for their future.

———

Until the late eighties, small family-run, general and convenience stores dominated the retail business across the country. Most middle-class families kept a monthly tab at the grocery store, at the cut-piece cloth vendor, the tailor, the milkman, the bakery. Food, toiletries and other essentials were requested at the beginning of the month; other essential items like clothes and bread were picked up as and when required. The monthly account was largely settled at the end of the month when most households received the salaries. Of course, sometimes the expenditure exceeded the monthly budget – especially if there were guests at home, or a wedding in the family or festivals or on account of travelling – and the local shopkeepers, having known their customers personally for years, would allow the balance to be paid in instalments in the following months. But the early to mid-nineties was a period of great change in the country, and the buying paradigm shifted before the family-run businesses had a chance to recover or rethink. The big business houses had realized that the biggest profit margins were actually in retail, which they wanted to dip into. They already had the resources, and once they spotted the opportunity, the onslaught commenced. They priced the local shops out of business. Even the most loyal of clients couldn't resist the glamour of the new and flashy stores and the amazing discounts. And the mere buying for necessities morphed into something called shopping experiences.

Bipin Desai did not work at some chhota-mota kirana store, like his friend believed. He worked for RealStores: a large company that owned over thirty supermarkets in the state of Uttar Pradesh, and some more scattered across Delhi and Rajasthan. They sold everything from grocery, fresh produce, clothes, fashion items, toiletries, household goods, to electronics, and just about everything one could describe as consumer products. An average store had a footprint upwards of two thousand square feet.

Bipin started on the shop floor and worked in shifts. With his schedule changing on a weekly basis – early mornings, late nights – it was inconvenient for him to travel from Munirka at odd hours using public transport. Though his parents were reluctant to let him to move out before he got married, he convinced them it was temporary. In a couple of years, after he was promoted at work and posted to the head office in Connaught Place, he'd return home.

Although the pay wasn't to his satisfaction, he enjoyed his newfound independence. Moreover, it was a great learning experience in a newly blossoming industry. As part of the internship, he was posted in different branches of the business to learn about various aspects of retailing.

He missed his friends. Manasi was studying – or at least pretending to – and couldn't go out as often. Also, travelling to and from Noida took more than an hour so they only met when Bipin was in Delhi. Anuj dropped by occasionally for a day or two. It was clear he wasn't getting along with his father, but despite several efforts on Bipin's part, Anuj showed no interest in the hard grind of the shop floor: *It is not for me.*

———

It had been four years since college ended. Manasi had failed the IAS entrance examination twice out of the three sanctioned attempts, so after another failure, the far-fetched dream could be put to rest. Anuj, still unemployed, was living with his parents and the rift between father and son had only intensified since Mr Shastri's retirement. Bipin worked relentlessly and, although the salary increased over time, the promised promotion and move to the head office in Delhi never materialized. Every time, they made an excuse or found a better candidate or hired someone with better credentials. After a while he gave up, sent his resume to placement consultants and found himself another job. It paid better, and was based in Delhi.

Despite Bipin's promise to his mother to return home, he'd grown used to the independence and, once he was back in Delhi, he decided to continue living on his own. He found himself a *barsaati* in Greater Kailash I; the flat was small but he liked the locality. The new job was in the regional office of a global retail giant in Nehru Place, which meant he didn't have to work shifts. No odd hours.

However, he realized that one part of the equation had transformed in the last few months since he had been busy finding a new job: Manasi and Anuj had started dating. Despite fleeting envy – he had always believed he was the more suitable choice since he had a job – he was more upset neither of his two close friends had let him know about their relationship sooner. It took the two lovers a bit of cajoling to placate him, but in the end, it was Bipin who took them out for a celebratory dinner, since neither of the two earned a living.

'So what's the plan – when's the wedding?' Bipin asked as they raised their beers in toast. He hoped he sounded happy, and not bitter.

Manasi and Anuj looked at each other. Then she spoke. 'One of us has to get a job first.'

A perfect response, but unfortunately it was just that: a good response. Since their graduation from college, Bipin hadn't seen either of them seriously look for a job.

'And then we can toast with champagne.'

'Yeah!'

4

JAILBIRDS

'so ...'

Mercifully, SI Khan entered the room a little more elegantly this time – fortunate, since he carried an uncapped bottle of Thums Up, the contents of which would have otherwise landed on Bipin. The bottle appeared chilled; tiny droplets precipitating down its length. The condensation was attributed to thermodynamics, they had studied it back in college, but the actual reason escaped Bipin now, as he tried to rack his brains. Not that he cared or that it mattered.

Bipin wasn't wearing a watch, but he reckoned he had been left alone for another thirty minutes.

'What have you thought?' Arfy asked, handing the bottle of cola to him.

Bipin smiled and uttered thanks and after taking a few generous sips, placed the bottle on the table. He let the

gas settle in his stomach before picking up the Thums
Up again and swallowing some more. He was thirsty and
dehydrated. He had probably been sitting in this boiling
room for over two hours. He had been arrested around
eight-thirty in the morning, which meant it was around
eleven now.

'What's the time now?' he asked.

'It doesn't matter; you're not going anywhere and
neither am I, until you answer my questions!' SI Khan
guffawed.

Bipin took another sip. The inspector wasn't wearing a
watch either. He certainly knew the time but was ignoring
Bipin's question once again.

'Take it slow, sonny boy, or you'll soon ask to go to the
toilet. We will end up passing the whole day between your
cola-drinking and pissing, and then maybe at some point
you will get so exhausted from running between this room
and the toilet, I'll have to hold you to take you to do pee-
pee.' The inspector laughed, proud of his joke.

Bipin smiled again. Not because he found it funny but
he wanted to appease the clown.

'I can't ask you to pay for this bottle because I know you
aren't carrying *the* cash.'

'*The* cash?'

'The stolen cash, did you not get the joke?'

This inspector was a cartoon. Bipin looked up but said
nothing.

'I'll be back,' Arfy drawled in an accent that in his confused mind was meant to sound like that of Arnold Schwarzenegger.

Then he turned and left. It took him the best part of two minutes to secure the lock again.

Was there something wrong with this inspector? Was he drunk? Bipin wondered if he should try to sniff out any traces of alcohol on the inspector's breath the next time he came into the room.

5

JAILBIRDS

THE KEY TURNED IN THE LOCK AGAIN. THE DOOR OPENED and the smiling face of Arfy Khan reappeared. When he had been brought in, Bipin had expected some thickset, bull-necked, menacing police officer, but his luck had got him this clown of a police officer. His humour was irritating at times, but Bipin reckoned he'd be a lot easier to handle than a menacing one. Also, SI Khan seemed easier to manipulate.

'Do you want the other thing now?' he asked.

'What other thing?'

'The orange one ...'

'You mean Fanta?'

'Yes, or Gold Spot or Limca? Do you want that now or later?' Arfy asked, clearly as a conversation starter. He wasn't going to go out, run and get one even if Bipin nodded.

'No, thanks, I'm fine.'

'Now why don't you make me feel fine by telling me where you've hidden the cash that you stole and we can all go home and drink whatever cold drinks we want.'

'I don't know what cash you keep asking me about?'

'Funny, isn't it? Here you are completely unaware of some cash that went missing from your old employer, and then there is your friend who thinks you know—'

'Know what?'

'Know where the stolen cash I'm talking about is.'

'How do you know what my friend thinks anyway?'

'Because he said so.'

'Why don't you tell him to come and say that to my face? I'll tell you why – because you haven't spoken to my "friend" or anyone. You took a chance that I have close friends – everyone has – and you thought dropping a little nugget like that would get me talking about something I don't even know about?'

The inspector scoffed again. 'You guys are quite a handful, you are. You two got away with a really big loot. You planned exceptionally well, I give you that. But don't believe even for a moment that you're some slick operators who've got away with it.' Arfy leaned forward and placed his forearms on the table. 'You guys are *just* cowboys.' He let out a curt laugh and shook his head in disbelief. 'I'm quite confident that if Clint Eastwood came to hear of your daylight heist he'd offer you the royalties for a screenplay, and who knows you might even get invited to the Oscars with all their pomp and circumstance.'

Bipin stared at the inspector silently. He hadn't expected the inspector to know of Clint Eastwood.

'And by the way Atul was arrested ten minutes ago—'

'Who's Atul?'

'Atul Shastri, your friend, your partner in crime.'

'I have no friend by that name.'

'Wait a second.' Arfy opened the file, turned some pages, and then closed it. 'Anuj Shastri, right?'

'What happened to Anuj?'

'Exactly what I just told you, sonny boy. Anuj was arrested about twenty minutes ago, and that's where I went after giving you the cola bottle. He's in the other room now, singing like a canary.'

'What?'

'You think I just left you here because I had a leaking bladder?' He laughed again.

This inspector thought he was a riot. Bipin didn't make an attempt to laugh at his piss-poor joke.

'Where's the cash, sonny boy?' Arfy repeated, sternly this time.

'We ... er ... I don't know.'

'So you stole the cash – what was it, one, two crores and it walked out on you? Did it have legs to walk by itself or did it grow wings while it was with you?' He laughed again, even clapping his hands like he was applauding himself. If anything, he looked a near-complete bundle of buffoonery. Was he for real?

'I didn't steal anything. There must be some misunderstanding. We ... er... I—'

'Why do you always err with *we* and then change to *I*? Perhaps Alok stole the cash and you are getting implicated because of your friendship. Feel free to tell me if that's the case, sunshine ...'

'Who's Alok now?'

'Oh, he's the same guy, Alok Shastri, Atul Shastri, how does it matter? Didn't William Wordsworth say, "*What's in a name?*"'

So he had heard of Wordsworth too. 'I think you'll find that actually it was William Shakespeare who said it,' Bipin corrected.

'Whoever. He said, "What's in a name?" So how does it matter whose name I attribute that quote to? Isn't that the whole point of the citation?' The inspector let out a loud laugh at his own gag.

Wow! Now, that's reassuring, Bipin wanted to say but stopped himself. Instead he said, 'I want a lawyer.' He realized there was little point in arguing. It was best to segue into something more meaningful than locking horns with this clown.

'What?'

'I said, I want a lawyer.'

'Yeah, I heard that bit. You want to lawyer up now?'

'Yes.'

'Why? If, as you claim, you're not guilty of anything, why do you need a lawyer?'

'Because I think you're trying to railroad me into something I have no idea about.'

'Oh, really?' Arfy attempted a scowl, but it came out as a sarcastic smile at best. 'Where were you on Monday, January the thirteenth, between 10 a.m. and 3:30 p.m.?'

'I was at home.'

'Can anyone corroborate that?'

'I was with my friend. So they can, if you need them to.'

'Oh, I see,' Arfy said, but his demeanour suggested he didn't believe his quarry whatsoever. Things didn't appear to be going well at all, Bipin thought morosely.

'Which friend?' the inspector asked.

'I need a lawyer. I think it is my right to ask for one, isn't it?'

'You've been watching too much television. In my opinion, people who steal from others, people who injure and kill others shouldn't talk about rights at all. What about the rights of the people they hurt or cause damage to?'

'I didn't kill anyone.'

'You're saying you were only involved in the heist but you had nothing to do with the murder then? Is that what you're saying?'

For someone seemingly absent-minded, SI Khan was quick. Bipin realized he'd need to watch out.

'I'm not saying anything. For the record, all I'm saying is that I want a lawyer.'

The policeman got up to leave.

'And I want to meet Anuj.'

'And I want to be the queen of England,' Arfy retorted almost replicating Bipin's tone, a schoolboy glee in his eyes. 'I mean, do you really think the police cares what you want or don't want?'

'Okay, I just want a lawyer.'

'Do you have anyone in mind? Do you know a lawyer?' Bipin shook his head.

'Do you want me to call Akash Hingorani?'

'Who's Akash Hingorani?'

'He's the best defence lawyer in New Delhi. He's also the most expensive, I'm told, but I don't think you have to worry about the money – with a crore or two stashed away somewhere.' He smiled again. The inspector's smile was beginning to annoy Bipin, but a bigger frenzy was building up in his mind now, with the knowledge of Anuj's stupidity. Bipin had categorically told his friend not to leave the premises until he was back from the short shopping trip. Or not until Saturday evening if he didn't return. Or had he told Anuj Sunday? Nonetheless, why had the idiot stepped out today? Or had their so-called safe house been busted? No, it couldn't be. If the safe house had been busted, the police would have found the cash too. And the inspector wouldn't still be questioning them, Bipin thought with some relief.

'Okay, but once you get a lawyer, I cannot offer you any deals.'

'What exactly are you offering me now?'

'Tell me where you have hidden the stolen cash and I'll see what I can do to help reduce your prison time when we go to court. And maybe increase Anuj's jail time.'

'Now why would I do that?'

'How about to save your fat ass to start with?'

'I told you I don't know anything about the cash you're talking about.'

'Okay, what if I got you free tickets to the cinema theatre of your choice in New Delhi for a full year, how about that?'

Bipin sat like a statue although he found the inspector's offer quite funny under the circumstances.

'No? Okay. How about free cinema tickets for the whole year and a chilled bottle of Thums Up whenever you go there. Of course conditions apply: you cannot order more than two colas per show. Does that sound appealing enough?' He chuckled.

Bipin, notwithstanding his surroundings and the agitation building inside him, couldn't stop himself from laughing out loud.

'Okay, so Thums Up is what gives you a kick, that does it for you.' Arfy picked up the file and started walking away.

'Where did you find Anuj?' Bipin asked.

'No one, and I repeat, no one can stay hidden if I am looking for them.' Arfy said giddily. 'We picked him up outside Munirka DDA flats. More precisely, outside his wife's place. We had put the place under surveillance two days ago.' He smiled again, like he had won round one of some pissing contest, which he indeed had, thanks to Anuj's idiocy.

'If you don't want to pay for a lawyer, we can arrange a public defender.'

'Who's a public defender?' asked Bipin. He was hardly conversant with the terminology. He hadn't imagined he'd be arrested, let alone need a lawyer. Never thought it'd come to this.

'Someone who defends the public.' This inspector seemed to think he was a stand-up. 'A public defender is a free advocate provided to you.'

'Okay.'

Bipin watched as Arfy almost tripped and fell out of the room, locking him inside once again.

What was wrong with this guy? He wondered for a second but he had enough problems of his own to focus on.

Then he waited and waited for Arfy to return.

And then waited some more.

6

FREE BIRDS

WITH MANASI BEING UNSUCCESSFUL AT GETTING THROUGH even the preliminary examination for IAS, her father didn't see much merit in postponing the search for prospective grooms. She was over twenty-five, and girls from good middle-class families were supposed to be married by then. Manjula had had both her kids by the time she was twenty-four.

He couldn't believe his ears when Manasi told him she was in love with a useless, unemployed friend from college. He had known Anuj and Bipin for quite some time now; if she had said she wanted to marry Bipin, he would have still understood. After all, the boy had a decent, stable job in Delhi. He made a living. But Anuj? *Hare Krishna*, the guy had no job, no future and – from what he knew – an attitude. Privacy for residents in the Munirka DDA flats was next to impossible. Everyone knew each other's business. Anuj had been written off as hopeless by most, partly due to his father's continuous whining and ranting about his son at the local tea vendor and barber, or whenever he ran into another public-sector retiree in the corridors. If a father didn't have any confidence in his own son, who else would?

And then, out of all the eligible bachelors in Delhi, Manasi had fallen in love with that idle boy. What was wrong with his daughter?

'Are you out of your mind?' he asked. 'He doesn't earn a single paisa.'

'What's money got to do with love, Pa? Money isn't everything ...'

'It's not everything, but it's one of the most important things to survive in this world. Where is he planning to take you – to stay in his parents' apartment and live off Mr Shastri's pension?'

Manasi stayed quiet. It was best to let her father let off steam once and for all.

'Where will he keep you, what will he feed you? You cannot survive on love alone!'

'We'll find a way.'

'It's easier said than done. Have you even thought this through?'

'I'll pass the IAS exam next time and then we can be out of your way.'

'It's not about getting out of our way, Manasi, it's about your life, your future and what you want to do with it. We are not your enemies, we are your parents, your well-wishers, *Hare Krishna*.'

'He's right, Manasi.' Mrs Upadhaya, who had stood like a sculpture beside father and daughter the whole time, finally broke her silence. 'You need to look at the long term—'

'And I am looking at the long term. If I pass the exam and get into the civil services we can have a future together, can't we?'

'And him? What will he do? Live off the money you bring in?' Mrs Upadhaya asked.

'What's wrong with that? Haven't you lived all your life on the money pa brought in—'

Manasi's mother slapped her across her face. 'Thankless child,' she said, bursting into tears, and walked out of the room. End of discussion.

———

'Romeo-Juliet, Laila-Majnu ... oh my dear god!' Mr Shastri was furious when Anuj told him about his romantic liaison with his college friend and neighbourhood girl.

Anuj hadn't wanted to tell him, but he didn't have a choice. With the growing pressure on Manasi to get married, he had to either acknowledge their relationship to his parents too or watch her marry someone else.

'Your son's gone mental, Shanti,' Mr Shastri yelled and looked from his wife to his son and back. 'He wants me to go to Mr Upadhaya's house and ask for his daughter's hand in marriage for a man who is good for nothing. He sits idle all day long building castles in the air, and now wants to bring us another mouth to feed.'

'Don't talk like that,' Shanti said. 'He will get a job. It's not like he's not trying—'

'Trying! Ask him when was the last time he applied for any job?'

'There've been no jobs that match my qualifications,' Anuj responded.

'If we go by your logic, I think we will have to wait for a job in the Rashtrapati Bhawan to come by. Because anything else will be a big step down for you, won't it? We wasted all that money on your education. Just my luck to have a son who's nothing but a freeloader.'

'So what do you want me to do – start sweeping the streets, become a janitor? Or become a clerk in some government office, like you?'

The last sentence, it looked like, was too heavy for the old camel's back.

'Look at his audacity, Shanti. He's mocking me. He's referring to my life's work like I was some menial janitor when he cannot even secure a basic job. All this while living off me!' he yelled. 'If I didn't keep you in my house, give you food, you'd be on the streets begging and stealing. Go out and earn your own bread, then come and talk back to me, you ungrateful scoundrel.'

Neither Shanti nor Anuj spoke. They had had similar fights before, but this was the first time Anuj had retaliated. It was best to let the storm pass.

But it didn't pass.

'No, this is it,' Mr Shastri continued. 'Today is Wednesday. I want you out of my house by Sunday. Pack your bags, take whatever clothes and belongings you want and get out of my life ... don't ever dare to show me your filthy face again—'

'Please think, Anuj *ke* daddy' Shanti intercepted, 'where will our poor boy go?'

'I don't know and I don't care. He can dig up a hole and live in it. I cannot allow him to subject himself to the humiliation of living off the pension of a public-sector clerk ... you cannot imagine how much he has hurt me today.'

'Please ...'

'No, Shanti, I've had enough. We cannot live under the same roof. It's either him or me. One of us has to leave the house. I'm not throwing him out right away, for which this ungracious boy should be thankful. I've spent my life supporting this rascal ...'

'Now get out of my sight, you wretched bastard,' he shouted and stomped into his bedroom, slamming the door shut.

———

Bipin loved his friends. They had certainly spent enough years together now to understand each other's problems, and like all friends, support one another. And since the three had invariably distanced themselves from the others, they did not have many other friends. At least, not as close.

But what Bipin hadn't accounted for was his two friends turning up at his doorstep to live with him. With neither of the two lovebirds earning a living, it was clear this was not a temporary arrangement. He understood their plight despite the other two not being in the least concerned that he too, at some point in the near past, had loved Manasi and seriously considered proposing to her. He hadn't done it in time, and the result was that his two best friends had become soulmates and he, a spectator. But that was water under the wobbly bridge of their friendship now – him not expressing his love could only be a result of him being in two minds: he was nervous and uncertain; he had held back until it was too late. But all the emotional turmoil aside, how was he supposed to house two additional people in a barsaati? A barsaati – literal translation: raincoat – was nothing more than a small, crudely built shanty a lot of house owners in Delhi had constructed on the rooftop to rent out to singles. Some of them were in better shape than others, but the one Bipin lived in had a barely fifteen-by-fifteen-feet floor space that included a living area, a kitchenette, place for a single bed, and a toilet-cum-shower behind a screen. Of course, he had access to the entire roof terrace. In the summers, one could sleep outdoors, but during winter the outdoor space was useless after the sun set.

The lovers needed space. The issue of privacy could be well taken care of when he went to work in the day. But this meant they would be using his bed for all kinds of intimacies. It was bizarre to say the least – the leftover odours of lust would haunt him at night. And the lingering smell of Manasi would bother him, but he would bear that. After all, that's what friends were for.

But how would he bear the expenses of two other adults? He had a decent salary, but there was rent, office clothes, transport, food, toiletries, and other sundries. Living in a metropolis like Delhi was expensive. One couldn't survive on thin air. He could live on his salary as a single person, not luxuriously but comfortably. Sharing the same paltry pot with two other mouths meant a slow and painful return to the days of penury. Not any better than his father working, and his mother and he living off his meagre salary. But it was different for his father. His father had married his mother and sired him. He had been prepared for the responsibility he was taking up. But Bipin hadn't volunteered for this arrangement, had he?

But every time he thought of bringing it up, he decided that they were his friends, and they were in trouble. That's what friends did for each other. He was happy to help but he was worried about *how*. And for how long? He had been in this job less than a year and changing jobs too often didn't look good on a resume, he was told. Recruiters preferred their employees to commit to the organization and job, not jump around at the first possible opportunity and ergo, he had to continue in the same job for another eight to nine months before he could even start looking for other jobs. Besides, he had begun to enjoy his current job: he was learning different facets of the business world. However, expecting a salary hike in the current company was out of question. There would be a year-end increment but for one, it was four months away, and two it would be a measly sum. In most companies he'd worked, the salary rise barely took care of the continually rising inflation. So, in effect, the buying power remained constant; maybe it rose by an insignificant two or three percent, which in his case, was enough to splurge on an expensive bottle of perfume, but not enough to indulge or pay for two extra members in the household.

Business? What if they got into some business, started a new venture? He sometimes thought about the possibilities when he lay alone at night in bed knowing the lovers were humping like bunnies on the terrace under the moonlit sky. Some nights if he peeped out, he could see them. Naked sweaty bodies, squirming and crying in ecstasy; however, each time he watched them and tossed off he felt like he was a perverted voyeur pleasuring himself by prying on his own friends. The remorse made him empathize more, think more about how all of them could get out of the mess his friends had created for him. He knew they'd have to do something. But what? Starting a business would require funds. Where would the investment come from?

And could these two – who'd never worked a day in their lives – actually get a job? Could, at least, one of them share the burden of expenses?

Days turned to weeks, and then months. The lovers seemed to be getting comfortable with the arrangement. They fucked each other's brains out during the day, and waited for their friend in the evening. To their credit they took over cleaning the room and cooking the dinner. They even did the laundry and ironed his shirts for work. Despite his initial hesitation, and the drain on his earnings, the communal living wasn't as much an interruption to his routine as he had feared. However, the arrangement had begun to eat into whatever meagre savings he had accumulated over the past five years. They were spending more in a month than he brought in. Once his savings ran out, the salary just wouldn't sustain three people. He did some quick maths and reckoned he had another three-four months. Maybe five, if they started skipping breakfast and survived on just boiled rice and salt and onions for dinner.

'Can't you steal some food from the aisles at the grocery store where you work?' Anuj asked innocently, but he sounded serious.

'I no longer work at a retail company on the shop floor, remember?'

'Oh, yeah, just when we needed you on the shop floor ...'

Despite his annoyance, Bipin let the comment pass. For a moment, he had almost barked: *why don't you stop resting your stupid ass and do something about it then?* But he knew it wouldn't do any good. If anything, it would destroy their relationship forever. Isn't that what Anuj's father had said? Anuj wouldn't be able to take a similar blow again.

There had to be a way. They couldn't be in the dumps all their life. There had to be a way up.

But he couldn't be more wrong.

———

'You know Bipin loved you too,' Anuj told Manasi one day, out of the blue. They had never discussed this before.

'What are you saying?'

'Don't pretend to be so shocked like it never occurred to you?'

'Of course not.'

'Liar.'

'How would I know if he's never told me or expressed it?'

'Well, it's written all over his face, his expressions when he looks at you.'

'Come on, Anuj. Bipin has been a friend for as long as you and I've known each other. I don't think he harbours such feelings towards me. You're behaving like a jealous lover.'

'I'm not jealous at all. I said he *loved* you, not loves you. I bet he had all the feelings for you that I had, but just like you said he's been our friend for so long I don't think he harbours any intimate or malicious feelings now.'

'Intimate feelings for me, I can understand,' Manasi admitted coyly, 'but why would he hold any kind of malice towards me if, as you claim, he loved me in the past? What have I done to turn his love into hate?'

'Not towards you, sweetie. The malicious feelings, if any, would be targeted at me.'

'You're just imagining it. He is so caring that he's opened his home and welcomed us to live with him, and you think he has some grand cunning plan to target you with his latent hatred?'

'Oh, when did I say that? I said he *does not* harbour any ill feelings towards us.'

'OK, if you say so, but I think you are the one who's feeling insecure because you see him around us all the time. You've convinced yourself using some bizarre, convoluted logic that he's intimately interested in me.'

'Shouldn't I be concerned when you just admitted that you know he has had intimate feelings for you?'

'I never said anything like that, you're just twisting my words,' Manasi was appalled.

'What did you mean then?'

'I didn't mean anything. I was only extending your logic to say if – and it's a big if – *if* he ever had romantic or physical interest in me. I didn't say he had any such feelings or he ever expressed them to me or any such stupid thing.'

'So you regret that he never explicitly voiced his feelings for you?'

'Anuj, I think you're making a mountain of a non-existent molehill.'

'Oh, really?' Anuj smiled slyly.

'I thought you were joking in the beginning, but you seem to be getting serious about this every minute. There was never anything between Bipin and me, nothing ever happened, nothing would happen … Happy now?'

'I am, but you sound unhappy by the sound of it.'

'Oh my god! I'm sorry, but I don't want to discuss it anymore.' Manasi turned away.

'I was only saying—'

'Shut up, Anuj.' She turned around to face him again. 'I do not want to listen to such nonsense again. Ever. If you ever mention anything like this again, that'll be the end of us. I hope I'm very clear. You're not only blaming your own friend for being nasty, you're also accusing me of being characterless, and that is not acceptable.'

'I'm sorry, I really am, Manasi.'

'OK, let's not talk about this anymore.'

'Talk about what?'

'I love you.'

'I love you too, Manasi. I love you more than you love me.'

'So, let's start another argument on this now?' Manasi quipped.

'I don't see why not? But on a serious note, I can't live without you.'

'Neither can I.'

7

JAILBIRDS

IT SEEMED LIKE A LIFETIME BEFORE BIPIN HEARD THE key turn again. He had no idea what the time was now. With no watch the best he could estimate was four, maybe five hours since he had been brought into the police station, booked, printed and sent straight to this room. There had been no conversation with those arresting him; the uniformed policemen had been brusque, but not abusive. He, going by the plan made with Anuj, hadn't initiated a dialogue out of fear of spilling any information that the police could use against them. A lot of times, the guilty couldn't stop themselves from talking about their innocence with such zest that the truth inevitably slipped out. Staying quiet was the safest option. He had told them his name when they had asked, and that was that.

SI Arfy Khan was back with a man wearing a black coat and white cotton trousers in tow. The lawyer. Tall and skinny, he looked like he had escaped some famine-struck country and walked barefoot a thousand miles, to defend Bipin. But his eyes were bright. Something in his demeanour exuded confidence. Whether that confidence was genuine or a sheer facade remained to be seen.

'Meet Advocate Mr Sriram Sharma,' Arfy introduced the man in the coat.

'Hello.' Advocate Sharma extended his hand and Bipin shook it. Firm handshake. Deep baritone. Bipin reckoned he'd be over fifty-five for sure. Sharma's coat was cotton too, starched and ironed well with the sleeve crease sharp enough to cause a paper cut. The white shirt was clean too. He looked like someone who had the experience to get Bipin out of this mess.

'Thank you, Mr Sharma.'

A glum-looking constable came in with another steel chair and placed it on Bipin's side for Advocate Sharma to rest his bony ass.

They heard Arfy slump into the chair and looked at him.

'What would you like to know; where do you want me to start, Mr Sharma?'

'It would be very helpful if you could tell me the charge against my client, Mr Khan?'

'Charges, Mr Sharma, charges. Plural. IPC Section 320, 390 and 299: Robbery, Grievous Bodily Harm and Culpable Homicide. I'm sure I can find some more that would stick; not sure espionage fits in, but I can always check – he had inside knowledge of the money since he robbed his employer ...' Arfy looked up, daring Bipin to contest and correct that it was his ex-employer. Until now, the accused had maintained that he knew nothing about the robbery. But Bipin didn't flinch.

'And you have evidence implicating my client?'

'Oh, yes, tangible evidence that places your esteemed client at the scene of crime beyond reasonable doubt. Enough proof to get a conviction, Mr Sharma.'

'Alright, Senior Inspector Khan, I need time alone with my client to confer if that's okay with you, please?

'Of course, take your time. I'm in no rush and your client isn't going anywhere ...' With this, he winked at Bipin like they were sharing a private joke.

A clown!

Arfy got up – thump; he seemed to have stubbed his toe against the steel leg of the table.

Good, thought Bipin.

'Mr Sharma, just one request if you may, please.'

'Definitely, anything I can do.'

'Could you kindly explain to sonny boy here ...' he gestured towards Bipin, 'that when he goes into the showers in the jail tomorrow morning, he shouldn't drop the soap ...?' Then he clapped, chuckled, and turned to leave. The policeman's banter would have been hilarious had they met in a different place in different circumstances. But Bipin was in no mood whatsoever for humour at this moment, not when he had been arrested for the heist of over one crore rupees.

'He thinks he's a riot, but he's getting on my nerves,' he said as soon as the inspector left.

'Hold on a minute,' Sharma said and pointed towards the red light. It went off after a few seconds. 'Never, ever make the mistake of uttering another word while this red light is on; the words and conversation will get recorded, understand?'

'Yes, sir.'

'And regarding the inspector, it's better he's funny and not intimidating, trust me. Now tell me everything.'

'Sure, where do I start?' Bipin sounded resigned.

'Well, the beginning is always good ...'

So Bipin started talking. And he told his lawyer the truth. After listening to the whole story, the defence advocate thought for a minute before speaking. 'One crore, wow! That's a lot of money.'

'Yes, sir.'

'And you still asked for a free lawyer?'

'I don't know anyone, so I didn't know what to do.'

'Well, I'll never make the kind of money you have. I mean I am a poor lawyer, but I will still fight for you. But if you want, I can get you a really hotshot lawyer who will take a lot of fees ... it's still not late if that is what you want.'

'Mr Sharma, how complicated is this case for you to handle?'

'It's quite simple really, but I won't earn anything from it. But some other lawyer can if you hire them.'

'I can pay you too.'

'It's not the norm, but some clients do offer to pay, you know ...'

After another ten minutes of mindless conversation, Bipin realized that Sharma wanted a share of the booty.

'How much will make you happy?'

'Five lakhs.' Sharma didn't need to think.

Bipin calculated quickly. They had over a crore and fourteen lakhs, so even if he paid five to the advocate, Anuj and he still had over fifty lakhs left for either of them. More than enough.

Although the public defender was paid by the state, they agreed that Anuj would pay the lawyer five lakhs if and when he got him out of this police station.

———

'And they've arrested Anuj as well ...' Bipin told Sharma after the deal was sealed.

'I know, I've been told. But I doubt your friend is "singing like a canary" as the inspector put it.'

'Thank god for that. I had specifically told Anuj not to step out of the house, but he's not very sharp. When I didn't return in an hour or two, he must have stepped out to see his wife. She's pregnant, but it's still extremely foolhardy.'

'Hmm ...'

'Can we not pay this clown inspector some money and get away?'

'You think I didn't think of that? Please don't make the mistake of offering him a bribe or he'll further charge you under Section 171B. Don't even think about it. He might be a clown, but I know that he's not corrupt. He's got loads of ancestral property and wealth, so I would advise that you don't even bring it up.'

'Shit!'

'Yes, mega shit, and besides, if you were involved in a robbery of twenty thousand rupees one could think of paying off some lowly constable maybe. But this is a case of grand larceny – a crore and some change.' Sharma's eyes bugged out at simply the mention of the amount. 'So on the whole you're in deep waters: you bit off a lot more than you can chew and then the heavens served you a bad deal – your case file is unfortunately with one of the most honest police officers in the area. You cannot buy him off and you cannot intimidate him even if you had contacts. By the way, do you have any political affiliations or contacts to whom we might be able to reach out?'

'I don't know anyone remotely important.'

'Too bad. Anyway, what have you told the inspector so far?'

'Nothing of consequence.'

'What do you mean by that? How can you be sure – you don't know which clues he's searching for, do you?'

'I mean I've said nothing.'

'How long have you been here?'

'Since the morning. I got arrested sometime around eight-thirty. What time is it now?'

The lawyer glanced at his old HMT Janata Deluxe, which, to Bipin, looked like the best watch money could buy right now.

'It's ten minutes past two now. Have you had something to eat since morning?'

'No, just water and a bottle of Thums Up, which he made a big fuss about.'

'Okay, then, let's get you something to eat first, and then we'll talk.'

'I want to get out of here,' Bipin almost pleaded.

'Rest assured, I'll try my best, don't you worry. Now, I'll try to arrange food for you.'

'Thank you.'

The advocate stood up and knocked at the door but Bipin didn't get to see who opened it.

Having spent the entire day in the sweltering interrogation room, Bipin suddenly realized he hadn't eaten anything. He had left home at eight thinking he'd be back in thirty minutes to eat breakfast, but the next thirty minutes had changed the course of the day, and maybe his life. If only Anuj had listened to his advice and not left the house.

8

FREE BIRDS

Bipin would never forget that particular Thursday evening. He had returned home after work to find Manasi and Anuj talking animatedly like they had won a gold medal at the Commonwealth Games. Or maybe even at the Olympics.

'You won't believe it,' Anuj started.

'Believe what? Have you won the lottery?'

'Not that; don't you ever think of anything but money?'

Yes, how about you making some money for a change?

'What is it then?' he enquired.

'You tell him.' Anuj turned to Manasi.

'No, you tell him.'

'No, you …'

'No …'

'Come on, guys, stop acting like schoolchildren and tell me about this unbelievable news.' If there was a trace of annoyance in Bipin's voice, it either went unnoticed or was ignored by the lovebirds. They stood gazing into each other's eyes with such intensity that the rest of the world could have ceased to exist and it would not have mattered. Until of course, hunger pangs resumed and someone – meaning Bipin – would have to work his ass off to buy them dinner.

'Manasi is pregnant. Isn't that great?'

Great! Great? Were these two creatures, his two best friends, some kind of morons? Couldn't they work out that it was financially impossible for their friend to support them? Who would bear the expenses of the pregnancy, the delivery, the hospital, and then the baby? The diapers, the baby's medicines, her tonics, her food ... God!

'Wow!' was all that came out of his mouth.

'What an achievement!' Anuj looked overjoyed, with eyes brimming.

Achievement? Guys, you've been screwing each other's brains out every day, and every night – did you not pay attention in the biology class? Two young and healthy adults copulating continuously without using any protection were bound to reproduce another human being. It's not an achievement; there are no Olympic gold medals for this ... this is simple biology.

Bipin nodded, but perhaps his expression belied his supposed joy.

'What's wrong, Bipin? Are you not happy that we are going to have a baby?' asked Anuj.

'Of course, I am happy, but—'

'But what?' Manasi looked at him askance. 'Something

wrong?'

'No. I was only wondering how your parents would react?

'Why? Do you think they would react adversely?'

'Because you two aren't married, that's why the thought came into my mind. Sorry I didn't mean to dampen the joy.'

'I understand where you're coming from and I'm a bit worried too, but not too much,' Manasi announced. 'Marriage is nothing more than a mere legal attestation of our love, a document, and we are going to get married, eventually. It's just a matter of time.'

Everyone's a wise-ass philosopher!

'I know but still ... you know how the society reacts to such matters. I mean not everyone is as broad-minded as the three of us here, people won't be as accepting of a child out of wedlock. And think of your parents – I mean, they will come to know sooner or later – sooner rather than later I think, and what will they think? They might get to hear all kinds of rubbish from their so-called friends.'

'You have a point.' Manasi seemed to accept.

Good!

'I think the least you can do is to tell your parents, and let them arrange some kind of a ceremony and get you two sorted.'

'I'm not going back to my father's place. If getting married is essential, then we will get married, and you shall be our sole witness. But we will all stay together.'

Fuck me!

This wasn't going the way Bipin had imagined. 'But—'

'Is there anything else?'

'Anuj – we have no experience; how will we know how to look after Manasi in the delicate state she's in?'

'No one knows that before it happens, do they? We'll consult the best doctor and go along with their advice.'

'What about the money?' There he said it.

'What about it?'

'I mean I'd love to take care of you two, and the baby but I am already stretched. I've been dipping into my savings, and to be honest I have only a few months of extra cash left.'

'You mean we are spending more than we earn in a month?' Sherlock had eventually worked it out.

We *earn in a month? We? Wow!*

'Look, I don't mean to cause distress to you two – I know you are going through a rough patch, but I thought it was best to share the financial position of *our* household.'

'I'll get a job.'

Good luck with that. 'Where? Have you thought about it?'

'No, but I'll do anything to share your burden to support Manasi and our child.'

The discussion continued while the three cooked rice and lentils. Manasi was tired and wanted to rest. Considering she was three-months pregnant, Bipin asked her to take the only bed in the barsaati, while the two guys could sleep outdoors from now on.

As they lay under the open sky, Bipin once again suggested that Manasi and Anuj seek blessings from their parents. Besides the financial and psychological support, it was the right thing to do. Parents generally forgave their children when a grandchild was on the way. 'You know what they say: the interest is always better than the principle,' Bipin quoted. Discerning the dumb expression on his friends' face he explained, 'the grandparents love their grandchild more than their own child.'

'Why?'

'I don't know, but that's how it has always been.'

'So you think we should go back?'

Eureka!

'Not go back, but if I were you I'd definitely let them know ASAP.'

Then maybe they will drill some sense into you two. Maybe you might work and make some money to bring up your child?

Bipin was irritated. But he also had intermittent pangs of guilt. His friends were ecstatic; they were having a child together. What could bring more delight than that? And here he was, being petty, fretting over fiscal repercussions that might burden him. So what if he used up all his savings on his friends for the time being? What had he saved for that could be more important than bringing up a child? He was conscious that his behaviour – since the time he had mentioned money – had put a damper on his friends' happiness. Manasi and Anuj had looked glum since he had revealed the state of his depleting reserves. He was conscious that he should take a step back.

'Go and seek their blessings at the very least. One step at a time, let's see what they have to say.'

'I think that's a good idea,' Manasi concurred.

'Anuj – I love you both. I don't have many friends, you know.'

'We have none either, and you know that. That's why we came to you when my father threw me out of the house. You're family to us. We talk about you all day when you're gone.'

If you talk about me all day then who the eff has been screwing? Shut up, Anuj!

'I know. So, please don't think I meant anything when I said we were low on finances. We'll work something out, don't worry about that.'

'But I was serious earlier, Bipin. I know I have to find work. Some work, any work. I'll go and ask local businesses around if they need any unskilled labour. I've to start somewhere – I'll pick up skills as I go along. For now I'll take up any kind of apprenticeship; I'll learn and also make some money. What do you think?'

Bipin didn't say anything, a wave of relief washing over him, since he knew he couldn't speak without letting his friend know that he was choking on emotions. When Anuj didn't hear anything back for a few minutes, he said goodnight.

On Friday morning, when Bipin was woken by the warmth of the sun on the terrace, Anuj had already slipped indoors. As he started getting ready for work, the lovers announced that they had decided to pay heed to his advice. They were going to visit their parents and break the news of Manasi's pregnancy.

A group hug followed.

'Thank you,' Manasi murmured. Unlike Anuj, she had left home on her own accord. She felt no hesitation in visiting her parents; on the other hand, Anuj had been unwilling, but a lecture from Bipin had made him appreciate that the circumstances had changed and maybe – just maybe – his dad might relent and welcome him back. Who knew?

However, there was no expectation that the parents might want to support them in their decision or even be willing to pay any bills.

After a few minutes, Bipin was also made aware that his advice was taken heed of with a condition: he would have to accompany them on Saturday.

'We are in this together, aren't we?' Anuj asserted.

Together? Three-gether? All together? How?

'Sure.' Bipin didn't see a point in arguing. He'd go with them, visit his parents too. Anyway, it had been a while.

When Bipin returned from work that evening the

couple was jubilant all over again. Apparently, there was another piece of good news waiting for him.

'This news will blow your mind,' Manasi exclaimed.

Twins? Triplets? Quadruplets? God, please ...!

'What is it?'

'You tell him.' Manasi turned to Anuj.

'No, you tell.'

'No, you ...'

'No ...'

Bipin wanted to bang his head against a wall.

9

JAILBIRDS

ADVOCATE SHARMA RETURNED AFTER WHAT SEEMED like another lifetime to Bipin, although he'd only been gone for twenty minutes according to his HMT. He carried four samosas wrapped in old newspaper and placed in the world's thinnest, transparent plastic bag. Bipin could see that the newspaper inside had been completely saturated by the oil in the samosas. He also carried a bottle of cold Bisleri. Thank god!

'They're bringing in the tea,' he said as he sat down. Bipin could smell that the advocate had had a quick smoke too. The stench permeated the closed room.

'Did you meet Anuj?' Bipin asked, putting his hand into the plastic bag and grabbing a samosa. Seeing the food made him hungrier than he had realized.

'Wait a second.' Sharma looked at the red light on the camera; it was off. 'Remember the first rule I told you?'

Bipin nodded. Sharma was only protecting his interests:

the camera would capture anything they discussed. The police, by law, were required to switch it off to give privacy to conversations between a lawyer and his client, but accidents happened or were orchestrated by police. One had to be vigilant at all times. 'No, SI Khan is with him now, the door to the other interrogation room was locked. It's just on the other side of the corridor. Anyway, I don't think they will let me or you see him before the inspector is through with both of you.'

'What does that mean?'

'He intends to break one of you.'

'Break? Break how? What does that even mean?'

'Have you ever read game theory in school or college?'

'Yes, but what does that have to do with this?' Bipin realized he had already finished one of the samosas and half the bottle of water. He took another one out of the bag and bit into it.

'You've read the theory in books; this is its practical application.' Advocate Sharma gathered that he needed to explain to his client what Arfy was trying to do. He gave examples, explaining how the police used prisoner's dilemma to get information. 'What our dear Inspector Arfy is doing is interrogating both of you simultaneously. Since neither of you is telling the truth, the two of you are bound to contradict each other ...'

Bipin listened to his lawyer intently. He had finished the second samosa and was contemplating if he should go for another. The water bottle was practically empty.

'And besides contradicting each other, he will also try to misguide both of you by telling you things your friend might or might not have said. His intention is to turn you against each other, lose your cool, say something out of spite or offer evidence against the other. You have to remember not to give in to any of his tactics, alright?'

'Is this even allowed … legally, I mean?'

'Yes, divide and conquer – the British used it all through history to colonize the world. Even in India they practised it even before the phrase "prisoner's dilemma" was coined. They turned one king against the other and divided them so the subcontinent was easier to conquer.'

Bipin decided to go for the third samosa in the end.

There was a knock on the door. The constable came in with two cups of roadside tea in cloudy glass tumblers.

'Thank you,' Advocate Sharma told the constable who looked like he had never been happy his entire life.

'Could I get some more cold water, please?' requested Bipin.

The constable gave Bipin a stern look like he wanted to kick the suspect in the bollocks for making him run errands. 'Okay,' he said, walked out and slammed the door shut.

'As I was saying, you need to be vigilant, weigh every word before you speak. Many hardened criminals have fallen for this trick. People who have no intentions of divulging any information, but they slip. Hours of frustration, sitting alone and waiting in a hot room like this,' Sharma rolled his eyes to accentuate the point, 'can make a person commit mistakes, and then you are told – even though you have no way to confirm it – that your own friend or partner is ready to give evidence against you, stick a dagger in your back. Do you see what I mean?'

There was a knock on the door again.

The same constable came in. He was obviously not pleased to carry water for them.

Bipin had an eerie feeling that the constable had spat in the water, but he muttered thanks and took a sip anyway. He was parched and knew he dare not ask for another glass of water. He hoped his lawyer would not drink his, so he might get the other glass too.

'Let me know when you finish the tea, we have to send the glasses back to the vendor,' the constable snapped and left the room banging the door even louder than the last time.

'Can't you talk to Anuj?'

'I don't think they will allow me to talk to your friend.'

'But you can surely talk to Anuj's lawyer. I'm hoping he's smart enough to have asked for one by now.' Bipin could feel sweat dripping from his body, but a shiver ran down his spine. He had always known Anuj was a little challenged in the grey cells department. 'Can we at least somehow suggest Anuj gets a lawyer in case he hasn't asked for one? Mr Sharma, my friend is not the sharpest tool in the box.'

'What do you mean?'

'Anuj is, how should I put it, a bit puerile, impulsive and a little hot-headed. And although I trust him like my brother, he might believe whatever nonsense the inspector feeds him, especially if he doesn't have someone experienced like you to guide him.'

'Oh, I see. I can certainly suggest a lawyer if he hasn't asked for one. If I find out he doesn't have one I can send one of my colleagues – someone trustworthy – to represent your friend, don't worry. Same fee for him, okay?'

'Of course.' Bipin could sense another five lakhs slipping away, but that wasn't something worth worrying about, certainly not at this juncture. Even after his and Anuj's fees were paid, they still had a crore to split.

'And if he's already got a lawyer could you find out who it is and confer with him on the side? It would be good to have an insight, isn't it?'

'I don't think the police will tell me but I'm sure I can find that out later.'

'Later? What do you mean later?'

'After I finish here today,' Advocate Sharma clarified.

'Do you mean you will not take me with you when you leave today?'

'I doubt that very much.' Sharma looked at his watch. It was close to four. 'My guess is that the police will wind up the day's proceedings soon. It depends on how long Arfy Khan wants to carry on. My guess is, given that they are all short-changed on resources, he's going to call it a day by five, five-thirty maximum. They'll put you in a holding cell and come back tomorrow to interrogate the two of you again. Unless—'

'Unless?' Bipin had never had any symptoms of high blood pressure and, as a result, he didn't know what it meant or how it felt. But he had heard people complain about it, his parents mentioned it sometimes, and now he thought he could feel his blood pressure was on the rise. But he felt woozy and lightheaded, his heart pounding against his ribcage. He had heard horror stories of first-timers like him getting raped and slashed in jails. He grabbed the last samosa and devoured it like his last meal on the planet. 'Unless ...?' He repeated.

'Unless one of you talks to Arfy, tells him what exactly happened, where the cash is, become a state witness and provide evidence against the other.'

'Why would either of us do that?'

Sharma explained that the inspector might propose an incentive, like a reduced sentence to whoever succumbed first to the deal offered by the police. Or if Arfy convinced one of them to betray the other by fabricating stories, he'd obtain the information he required to charge them. The advocate highlighted other similar scenarios, none of which boded well for Bipin or Anuj. He could only pray that Anuj wouldn't crumble under pressure before Sharma had made contact with the other lawyer. His mind returned to the holding cell where he would have to spend the night. His heart began drumming again.

'I don't think I will survive the night with other felons in the jail. I'm told there are murderers there.'

'I'll see to it that you get solitary confinement so no one bothers you.'

'You can do that?'

'I'll try my best. You don't have any past record, so I'm sure Arfy will agree.'

'Thank you, sir. Could you also ask them to put Anuj and me in the same cell so we can talk?'

Sharma's countenance revealed that his client had asked the most foolhardy questions of all times.

'Did I say something wrong?' Bipin asked.

'I just told you the police will not permit your lawyer to talk to your co-conspirator, they would not even tell me who his lawyer is because they do not want me to establish contact with either of them since it would lead to contamination of evidence. What are the chances Arfy would put both of you in the same cell all night to iron out your story?'

'I'm sorry. I get it now. I am just not myself today,' Bipin apologized.

'I can understand your state of mind. But you've got me now to think for you, so relax. May I suggest that when Arfy comes in next, you only answer his questions after I tell you to? Every time he asks you a difficult question, look at me. If I nod, respond. If I think the question is not appropriate, I'll intervene. If you are not sure about answering any question, ask for a timeout, saying you want to consult with me first. I'll ask him to give us time. That's your right. Trust me, if we play our cards right we can beat Arfy and his tactics. It's been done before, and it can be done again … now stop fretting, okay?'

Bipin nodded. Advocate Sharma appeared to have knowledge and experience. He seemed to know what he was doing, so it was best if Bipin let him take the lead.

'So your friend,' Sharma started after sipping the water. Bipin cursed himself for not going after it earlier. 'How much money does Anuj have?'

'I already told you how much we have, so why do you ask again?'

'No, I meant how much money, do you think, Anuj would have decided to spend on the lawyer?'

'I thought we agreed to the same amount as you – five lakhs, isn't it?'

'Bipin – listen to me first, don't answer my questions with another question, please.'

'Sorry.'

'I need to know if Anuj, like you, would have also agreed to sign up with a public defender or knowing that you guys have got loads of cash, he would have gone for some hot-shot lawyer?'

'You mean Akash Hingorani?'

'You *know* Akash Hingorani?' For a moment Sharma's eyes shone like someone had seen God or an angel. This Akash Hingorani must be some superstar lawyer.

'No, Inspector Arfy mentioned him so I remembered. But to answer your question, I don't know who Anuj would ask for. But how does knowing that help us any way?'

'It helps me in finding out who his lawyer could be. If Anuj has asked for a public defender then he should be someone I know so I should very easily find out who it is within a matter of hours. Once I know who it is, I'll reach out to him, lawyer-to-lawyer. I'll let him know your offer, and between the two of us we can work out how to play Arfy. It goes without saying that none of us – neither the lawyers nor you guys – would mention this little side deal to Arfy. He shouldn't even get an inkling that we are in cahoots. Only then do we get the upper hand.'

'Got you.'

'And I need to go out for a smoke from time to time, so whenever I go out, I can check on the other lawyer.'

'That'll be brilliant, Mr Sharma.' However faint, Bipin could see the proverbial light although he couldn't assess how long this wretched tunnel could be.

'Now let's wait for Arfy Khan. Remember, do not answer anything unless you get a nod from me, OK?'

'Yes, sir.'

As if on cue, there was a knock on the door. It was the dour constable again. He had come to take the glasses back. Bipin wanted to request more water but refrained. If he was going to spend the night in the lock-up, the last thing he needed was to antagonize the constable.

'Could you let SI Arfy Khan know that I'd like to have a word with him please?' Sharma was exceptionally respectful.

The constable looked at Sharma but said nothing. He stomped out and banged the door shut. Bipin noticed that the sound of the slam was a decibel or two higher than on the previous two occasions.

Sharma crossed his right leg over his left knee. 'As a matter of fact, it's good if Inspector Arfy closes early today. I'll get a chance to sneak out and put our little plan into action. Come tomorrow morning and Anuj's lawyer and I will both be well prepared, don't you agree?'

'Right, right.'

'And I also get time to think about what you've told me. Even if neither of you slip up or snitch on each other, we still need to come up with a plausible explanation for everything. I need to find out what evidence the inspector might dig up to come after you. There must be something that led him to you. He sounded quite confident.'

Bipin had been racking his brain since the morning, but for nought. The only thing he could think of was Anuj's driving licence, but he decided not to bring it up even with Sharma.

'All we need to do is to raise reasonable doubt in Inspector Khan's mind that this is maybe someone else's work. *Maybe* is the operative word here, and *maybe* is all we need. Unless the police are a hundred percent convinced it could be no one else but you and Anuj, they cannot charge you with the crime. They wouldn't even dare to file the case in the court.'

'Hmm ...'

'Let us wait for the inspector,' Sharma said after a brief recess.

And so they waited for another forty-five minutes before Senior Inspector Arfy Khan walked in, this time without losing his footing. But, worryingly, he had a 220-watt smile on his face.

'Hello, Mr Babul Desai—'

He had a momentary urge to yell and correct Arfy but he let it pass. What was even the point?

10

FREE BIRDS

THE SECOND PIECE OF GOOD NEWS OF THE WEEK THAT Manasi and Anuj eventually conveyed after finishing their quotas of *you-tell-no-you-tell* was definitely worthy of the happiness plastered on their faces. And no, it wasn't twins or triplets like Bipin had dreaded. Anuj had finally managed to get himself a job. It wasn't an office job, but he hadn't been looking for that in any event.

Two blocks behind Bipin's barsaati in GK I, there used to be a vacant plot that had fallen into some kind of family dispute. While the family members awaited the court's decision – it had been almost seven years since – a third person, called Munna ji had decided to capitalize on the situation. One fine morning, he had occupied a little corner of the plot and then gradually, like ground ivy, crept in and taken control of the entire eight hundred square yards. Soon, he set up a little motor repair shop there. Initially, the residents in the locality were hesitant to take their cars to him, but eventually came around to his shop for minor fixes. Munna ji was good and economical, and extremely friendly; moreover, the comfort of having a trusted mechanic in the locality to sort out minor automobile problems, without having to incur the exorbitant cost of branded garages, was welcomed. To make it stress-free for his clientele, Munna ji's garage was open twenty-four-seven, three-sixty-five days. It was hardly a bother for him, since he had just put up a temporary shanty, bribed someone to secure electricity and water and started living on the premises. Office-cum-home! Then Munna ji hired some help, and if possession was truly nine-tenths of the law, Munna ji had virtually become the owner of the plot. Even if the courts at some point in the future decided in favour of any of the disputed owners, the legitimate owner would find it practically impossible to shift Munna ji out without paying him a good amount for moving the business or retiring.

It was the well-known Munna ji's garage services that had hired Mr Anuj Shastri as an apprentice. Anuj would most certainly have been his first graduate recruit.

'But you don't know anything about motors.' Bipin was concerned. He was happy that his friend had decided to be responsible for once, but he hoped Anuj hadn't lied about his experience with motors to secure the job because he'd be caught out on the first day itself.

'Munna ji knows I'm a fresh pair of hands.'

Thank god for small mercies!

'There'll be on-the-job training on the shop floor, so to speak. Not very different from how you learnt retail at RealStores, I'd say. Only the size of the organization is different, and the industry.'

'I'm so happy.' Manasi's eyes were brimming with joy. Anuj had woken up to reality.

'I'm so happy for you two. But I really want you both to live with me as long as you please, and not leave me right away, now that you'll be earning and become independent.'

'Of course, we'll stay with you, where else will we go?'

A group hug ensued, including tears of joy. It even called for a small celebration – how far they had come in life, and how they had remained such good friends that they had become a family; a bit of an odd family, but still …

———

Saturday morning, they had first gone to see Manasi's parents.

Mr Upadhaya nearly had a heart attack or he feigned it brilliantly. He held his chest and went weak in his legs. Bipin rushed to assist him to the nearest sofa, and then rushed to the kitchen to bring him some cold water.

'Hare Krishna,' he uttered and closed his eyes like he was in actual physical pain.

Mrs Upadhaya, with Manasi still in her arms, was in a quandary: she didn't know if she should rejoice for her three-month-pregnant daughter's homecoming or start breaking her bangles if her husband happened to pass away from the shock.

'Why did I live to see this day?' Mr Upadhaya murmured after a short while. '*Hare Krishna.*'

If there was ever a moment to keep your mouth shut, it was now, but Anuj took it upon himself to convince Manasi's father. Wrong tactic, but there you go.

'But what is the problem, sir?'

'What is the problem?' Mr Upadhaya's tone was sarcastic, acerbic. Spittle flew out of his mouth in indignation. His eyes were bloodshot. If he could, he would have slapped Anuj or gouged his eyes out, but Mrs Upadhaya sat beside him, rubbing his arm to somehow calm him down.

'I am a Shastri, you're an Upadhaya; we're both Brahmins, so there should be no issue,' Anuj carried on regardless.

'Shut up, you rascal,' he screamed, and then turned to Bipin, 'you should have had some moral sense, some shame. Do you understand what being the father of a pregnant, unwed daughter means in our society?'

'But that's why we're here,' Anuj continued, 'to seek your blessings to get married, so that—'

'Now? You're here now, after you ... you ... you ... son-of-a-bitch have raped my daughter?' He almost choked on his words, gasping for breath.

'Raped?' Anuj looked aghast at the accusation.

'Daddy!'

'You ... you tart, you should have thought of us before you opened your legs for him. Shameless woman. They said *Kalyug* was coming soon, but I didn't realize it would be so soon! It's only 1996. And it didn't have to start from my home. *Hare Krishna*, it must be my sins from my previous life, my bad karma.'

Bipin repented. What had he been he thinking? Why had he come up with this bright idea to get the parents involved? This was not at all going down the way he had envisaged. Mrs Upadhaya's initial joy had dissipated too. Having an unwed daughter with a child wasn't something they could conceal in a middle-class neighbourhood. Even if Manasi and Anuj got married today, anyone could do the maths to uncover that she was pregnant before the wedding.

'*Hare Krishna* ... please leave us alone in our old age,' Mr Upadhaya implored with tearful eyes. 'We don't want anything from you, but please don't ruin our lives and our reputation by coming here with this bastard in your womb.'

That was it. There was nothing more for anyone to say. No other words were exchanged. Even Mrs Upadhaya didn't get up from her husband's side to say bye to her daughter; she sat there holding her husband's arm like a sailor held his oar. Manasi's waterworks started even before they got out of the apartment, it didn't seem they'd be stopping any time soon.

The scene at the Shastri home was no less melodramatic. Mrs Shastri opened the door and appeared happy to see her son return, and when she got the news of the grandchild she was over the moon and back in five seconds. She took Manasi in her arms and walked back to announce the news of the new arrival in the household to her husband.

But Mr Shastri threw a fit. 'As if it wasn't enough to feed one bastard, now he wants us to feed two bastards and his barefaced woman. Get out of my sight both of you, and you too.' He pointed at Bipin lest he thought he was welcome to stay back for lunch.

But how is Anuj a bastard if you're married to Mrs Shastri? Bipin thought, caustically. However, he kept quiet.

'Bipin, take us somewhere, we want to get married right now,' Anuj announced the moment they walked out.

Bipin looked at Manasi who was still in a state of shock at the behaviour of both sets of parents. She had expected some backlash, but certainly not something of this magnitude. Both her parents and Anuj's hadn't shown any compassion towards either of them.

'Anuj is right,' she softly said.

There was but one place left. It could be an equal disaster, but now that they were here it was worth a try. What did they have to lose?

'Why don't we go to see my parents? We'll tell them everything. They will probably be more dispassionate and maybe they could talk to your parents, and work things out. What do you say?'

'I think your parents should take us to some temple, get us married and give us their blessings.'

———

Mr Desai listened to the news of the morning's events at the two households and contemplated if he should get involved in the situation, which seemed dire. Should he play with fire? The Upadhayas and the Shastris had been their neighbours for years. He saw them almost daily on his morning walks; they even talked to one another about their kids sometimes. And this wasn't some transient accommodation for him: he had to live in here for the rest of his life. So would Messrs Upadhaya and Shastri. If he intervened and got their children married when their parents were against the match, they'd never forgive him, would they? He'd be seen as some kind of a traitor in the neighbourhood. However, the alternative was letting the young couple walk away and deliver a child out of wedlock when he had a chance to make matters right.

The living room was quiet like a coffin for a while. Bipin was glad that his father had stayed calm unlike the others, which brought some solace. He looked and saw his friends expectantly waiting for Bipin's father to speak although he seemed to have gone into some kind of a trance, thinking, meditating, perhaps waiting for manna to drop from the heavens.

'You should have come here first, and let me talk

to them,' he rendered his advice earnestly after he had digested all the information.

In retrospect it might not have been a bad idea at all. Maybe, as one parent to another, the conversation would have taken a different course. Perhaps one of the lovebirds' fathers might have been more inclined to heed advice from a peer. And if one of them got convinced, the battle would have been half won at any rate.

But it was too late now. One couldn't erase what had already occurred. From what Bipin had experienced in the morning, it was evident both Anuj and Manasi's fathers had already taken an obstinate stand. His own father was correct: changing their decision now would be twice as challenging. Pride, ego and all that shit.

'Please help us, Papa,' Bipin insisted.

'Let me think,' he said, got up and retreated to his bedroom like he would find the answers written somewhere under his bed maybe, or consult the Gita.

Mrs Desai went to the kitchen to make tea for all, taking Manasi along with her.

'This is what we'll do,' Mr Desai emerged after a brief fifteen-minute sojourn to his bedroom. Maybe he had a bonsai fig tree he sat under and attained awakening like Buddha himself, but he seemed a bit more poised and optimistic than he was when he had received the news, although there was no halo circling around his head. 'I have made a decision.'

Out of all the four present, Mrs Desai seemed the most eager to know what her husband had decreed. At the end of the day, his word had been no less than a commandment in the household for over three decades.

'We must surely get you married with our blessings. I'll call the priest at my temple and arrange for a simple ceremony for today or tomorrow, depending on the priest's availability.'

Nods. A wave of glee passed through the room.

'But …'

Everyone in the room looked at him to continue.

'Then you should go away from here for the time being. I'll talk to both your fathers, but we need a little time to make it right. It might take me a little while to convince them, you see. The situation isn't totally irretrievable. Quite frankly nothing is. You can even use spilt milk if you can get your neighbour's dog to slurp it. But this will take time. I can't promise if and when they will change their minds, but I'll try my best, I can promise you that.'

Anuj stepped forward and touched his feet. 'Thank you, uncle,' he said and embraced him. Manasi stepped forward but Mr Desai stopped her. 'Daughters don't ever touch feet, my dear.' He took her in his arms, along with Anuj.

For no apparent reason, soft blubbering abounded. Manasi, Anuj and Bipin's mother all had tears of joy or gratitude; it was difficult to tell. Bipin, not wanting to be a spectator, joined the tiny congregation of tearful celebrators. Why the hell not?

———

True to his word, Mr Desai spoke to a priest who was willing to come down to their apartment to carry out the simple ceremony, but Mr Desai put his foot down. It was enough risk that he was helping them get married without their parents' permission, he wouldn't chance his neck by arranging the service at his apartment. No way.

Temples around Munirka were a strict no-no. The last thing they needed was to accidentally run into someone from the neighbourhood. So they picked the Arya Samaj Temple on Gurdwara Road in Greater Kailash Part II. It wasn't too far since the bride and groom had to return to GK I anyway after the wedding. The priest did some calculations and suggested that Sunday was a better day for the young ones to tie the knot, so Bipin, Anuj and Manasi stayed the night at Bipin's apartment.

The wedding was the simplest of affairs. Bipin's mother decided which sari the bride would wear. She dressed Manasi up all by herself; there was no question of involving any neighbour. The whispers would travel faster than a Concorde and fly straight to Manasi's parents or Anuj's, which could lead to disastrous consequences.

Manasi looked very beautiful in the pink sari she wore. Although she still didn't have the bump, the radiance on her face made her extremely beautiful. For a second Bipin felt a pang of envy – she could have been his bride, this could have been his moment, but he blocked his injudicious emotions. They were his friends, he shouldn't ever look back at what could have been, he reasoned. But she was smouldering. Trying as hard as he could to stop them, images of her and Anuj making out on his roof terrace flashed before his eyes nevertheless.

Mr Desai had ordered two taxis. He insisted that both vehicles should have dark windows, and that they come as close to the exit as possible. The five members drove off from Munirka as clandestinely as a middle-aged man sneaking off to see his mistress.

The ceremony was short. Being an Arya Samaj temple, only four *pheras* were required, not seven. Which suited them, as time was of the essence here. Mr Desai liked being in command; he discharged his duties rather sincerely. He was elated to get the opportunity to do the *kanyadaan* – the sacred ritual. Since he didn't have a daughter he was in tears carrying out the emotional and sentiment-laden custom.

Mrs Desai wasn't taking her duties light-heartedly either. The parting at the temple was no less than a *bidai*, another customary affair. A lot of strangers in the temple had gathered to cry along to make it appear a lot more dampening than it should have been when saying goodbye to a one-day-old, borrowed daughter. But the sheer solemnity of the situation made everyone sentimental.

The little religious ceremony was followed by the distribution of sweets, since everyone sensed there might be no formal wedding reception. Not in the near foreseeable future, not until Manasi's and Anuj's parents agreed to accept the couple and be willing to bless them.

In the taxi back to Bipin's barsaati, the newly married couple sat in the rear holding hands. Bipin was happy, and so was the driver of the taxi who, surprisingly, had pulled out some of his old audio cassettes and played old Hindi wedding songs.

'*Mere haathon mein naun naun chudiyan hain*' was playing when they got down from the taxi and paid the driver a generous tip. Once inside the barsaati, the mood was mixed. Should they be happy they were married, or should they mope that their parents had abandoned them?

'He called my unborn child a bastard.' Anuj was clearly disturbed, and understandably so. Which parent would want to listen to that kind of abuse for their child, even if it came from their own parent?

'But you're married now so what your father said does not apply,' Bipin said, sensing Anuj was hurt and assuaged his friend.

'I don't know. What do you think the status of the child is if she or he is conceived before marriage but born after the parents have tied the knot?'

'Who knows—' Manasi said.

'And who cares?' Bipin completed Manasi's sentence. 'What matters is that you two love each other and you did what was right for you. Who cares what the rest of the world thinks or says?'

'You're right, I suppose.'

'Of course, he's right,' Manasi declared.

The discussions dragged on until late at night.

'Don't you guys have to go to work tomorrow?'

Realizing both Bipin and Anuj had work the next day, they wound up. Anuj was excited; it would be his first day at work – his very first day of work ever.

11

JAILBIRDS

'WELL, WE HAVE TO CLOSE THE PROCEEDINGS FOR THE DAY now,' Senior Inspector Arfy Khan announced after no one had corrected him for calling Bipin Babul.

Advocate Sharma looked at him askance. 'Why so early – it's only four-thirty.'

'I need to go and beg my superiors for my next quarter's budget, I'm sorry. You might think we only have to deal with criminals,' Arfy looked at Bipin for emphasis, 'but we have to also deal with our bosses. It's not as simple a job as it seems.'

Sharma got up. 'Could I speak to you in private for a moment, please?' He pointed towards the door.

'I don't see why not ...' Arfy said, and then turned to Bipin. 'And you, sonny boy, you will be our guest for the night. Constable Bhim Singh will take you to the holding cell. You'll be dined and given a bed to sleep on. Don't worry, it will all be on the government's tab. Free boarding for you tonight. Happy?'

'Could I share the cell with my friend Anuj please?' Bipin's words came out like he was on the verge of tears.

'Look at my face closely, sonny boy,' Arfy circled his index finger around his face and politely but sarcastically asked, 'do you see *chutiya* written anywhere?'

'No, sir.'

'Anything else?'

'Sir, why do I need to stay here tonight? Have mercy on me; I have Mr Sharma here who can vouch for me. I promise I'll return tomorrow morning for questioning, I will not run anywhere …' Bipin stopped mid-sentence; he realized how foolish he sounded with that request.

'That is such a brilliant idea, sonny boy! Maybe we don't need any jails in this country any more then. We can send all the prisoners home at night and wait for them to return for breakfast in the morning. It's such an innovative idea – I will suggest this to my boss in the meeting later this evening. Maybe you will get nominated for a "Boy Genius" award on Republic Day, who knows?' Arfy smiled; he didn't wait for a response from Bipin. He turned to Sharma and continued, 'When you return I'd like you to please explain to your client that this isn't exactly a Sheraton or a Hilton where he can check in and check out any time he likes or ask to share a room with whoever he fancies. Maybe next, he will ask for Sharon Stone in his cell.'

'I will talk to him, sir,' Sharma confirmed and headed out after Arfy, leaving Bipin alone.

Bipin could hear faint murmurs behind the door. There seemed to be an argument, and while there weren't any raised voices, Bipin could sense the discussion going back and forth like Sharma was asking for something that was being refuted by the inspector or the other way around.

Twenty minutes later Sharma returned to the room. The first thing he checked was the red light on the camera. It had been switched off.

'What happened?' Bipin was nervous since Sharma's face wasn't as buoyant as he had expected.

'Well, the good news is that I've convinced Inspector Arfy to arrange for a solitary cell for you. I put my foot down – told him that there is no way he can put you in a lock-up with murderers and other dangerous prisoners. You're what they call a first-time offender, so ... that part is sorted.'

'Thank you ... and the bad news ...?'

'But he isn't willing to cut any slack on anything else. He says Anuj has already got himself a lawyer, but he's adamant he won't reveal the name of his lawyer to me. He won't even tell me if Anuj has hired a premier lawyer or someone from the state's roster like me,' Sharma sounded cheesed off.

That didn't sound good. 'So, what do we do now?'

'I said *he* won't reveal the name to me. That doesn't mean someone else in the police station wouldn't.' Sharma paused for effect like he was on some television show. 'I can find someone who will be willing to give us the information once inspector Arfy leaves the premises. I need to get in touch with my contacts who will be able to find someone within this police station who'll agree to talk. For a price, of course—'

'Money is no problem, Mr Sharma, you know that.'

'Yes, I do know that, but you don't have access to any money right now, do you?'

'I can arrange it the moment I'm out of here, you know that.'

'But that depends on your release, which in turn depends on paying off someone *now* who can help us proceed with our little plan. It's a kind of catch-22, isn't it? Without money we lack the inside information, and without that, we don't have access to the funds, you see what I mean?'

'Hmm ... I'm sure you can think of something.' If only Anuj had stayed behind with the money, like they had discussed and agreed, they wouldn't be in this mess. Sharma could have collected the money from the safe house. But ... it was what it was. For all Bipin knew, Anuj had a valid reason for stepping out. He'd only know once they got out of this police station.

'I could borrow some money from people I know on short-term interest but you will have to pay them once you are out, and that would be over and above the fees we've already agreed. Would that be okay with you?'

'How much would it cost?'

'Since your friend Anuj has got his own lawyer it's only my share now – five lakhs – but I might need to spend another one lakh or so to grease greedy palms to get to the information we need on an urgent basis.'

What Bipin had heard about lawyers all along was indeed turning out to be true. Mr Sharma had him by his short and curlies; he had a nasty feeling that the piggish lawyer was conning him now – with the knowledge that Bipin had one crore stashed away. But he couldn't possibly think of an alternative at this stage. It was best to swallow his rising anger: antagonizing Mr Sharma would only make matters worse. The next question in his overheated, overworked brain was who he could ask Sharma to borrow money from, if he didn't want to incur interest? His father? How would the poor man arrange such a huge amount? And worse still – how would Mr Desai react when he found out Bipin had been arrested on a charge of robbery? He might have a cardiac arrest in shock. And his mother would cry her eyes out. Then, in his typical manner his father would blame her for bringing Bipin up badly and his mom would bang her head on the Godrej almirah. He could almost visualize the scene. No, he had no other choice, but maybe he could negotiate.

'That's a lot of money, isn't it?'

'It is but it's entirely up to you. You're my client, I'll do what you want me to do. I was only trying to be pre-emptive, like we discussed, so we can have our best shot tomorrow when we meet the inspector. But remember, it's *your* life we're talking about here. The money sounds too much, but don't forget I will need to contact as many people as I possibly can to dig up all these details for you, as we only have one night. The inspector will be back tomorrow morning. It's Thursday today, and I can bet Arfy will try to get you to court by Saturday morning. He can only keep you here, in remand, for a short duration, forty-eight hours. He will take you to court and once the court approves of the charges, you will go to jail—'

'You mean proper jail, like Tihar?' Bipin could feel his pulse rising, his stomach turning. He had never been so frightened in his entire life.

'I don't know which one, but yes, a proper jail. Your stay here at this police station is temporary.'

Shit! Shit! Shit!

Bipin couldn't speak. Suddenly, the money Mr Sharma had asked for seemed a trivial sum.

'And the money I've quoted – this one lakh – will need to be paid to all the contacts, and the person who will put his neck on the line to reveal the other lawyer's details. I know the amount sounds large, but the task ahead isn't as simple as you think. I'll need to engage a lot of trustworthy sources, and one has to pay for their time. Moreover, these people will need to work their asses off through the night, and they always demand a premium rate for anything that's time-critical and vital. I can promise you that not a single rupee of that sum will go into my pocket if you are concerned about it—'

'No, no ... no, I didn't mean that, Mr Sharma. Not at all.' Bipin unexpectedly felt guilty listening to Sharma's long spiel. He wondered if he had come across as rude, like he had questioned Sharma's motive or character. It was in his interest to apologize and make peace immediately. 'I'm extremely sorry if my question seemed accusatory, you don't have to explain. Like I already told you I'm in agreement with the costs you've indicated. Please forgive my stupidity. Just get Anuj and me out of this police station, please, in whatever way you think is right.'

'The money is for expenses, Bipin. I'll try and spend as little as possible, but you are a man of the world so you know that such expenses are without receipts – I mean I can't ask for a bribery receipt.' Sharma shrugged and passed a wry smile. *Take it or leave it!*

'I know.'

'Moreover, look at it this way – you saved five lakhs by not asking me to get a lawyer to represent Anuj. Your friend was smart enough to ask for one. Now, we don't know how much Anuj has promised the other lawyer.'

Bummer! Bipin could only hope Anuj hadn't promised more than he had to Sharma. 'I get it,' he uttered.

'I will leave after the constable comes to take you from this room. I'll walk out with you.'

'Wouldn't it be better if you left now and waited outside the building? I mean Anuj's lawyer should be leaving now too. There's a chance you will spot him and catch him right away.'

'I thought about it. But he's already left.'

'How do you know?'

'Inspector Arfy had packed up with Anuj before he came here to see us. Anuj has already been dispatched to the lock-up for the night. The reason we are waiting is because the same constable will return to take you in a while.'

'Oh …' Then Bipin asked: 'So there's a possibility I might accidentally be camping for the night in the cell next to Anuj's?'

'It's possible, but unlikely. Inspector Arfy isn't *that* stupid.'

'So you agree he *is* stupid.'

'Oh, he has a reputation. The commissioner of police abhors him, calls him a "village idiot".'

'So that's good for us, isn't it?'

'It should be. That's why I'm telling you that we should be putting in our best efforts tonight and, by tomorrow, this case could just go away. If we go as per my plan, Arfy won't have a clue. He'll be blindsided. We can win this.'

'I trust you completely.'

'Good. Actually the relationship with your lawyer should be no different from the relationship you have with your doctor. You must trust him completely and unconditionally. That's the only way it can work. We lawyers know the system well enough to play it to our advantage.'

'Of course, Mr Sharma.' Bipin realized he sounded ingratiating; so be it.

'The only advice I have for you is that you should relax. They will give you food – not Mughlai dishes, but they have minimum standards for hygiene – and you will have a safe place to sleep. Before you know the night will turn into day and I'll be back at your service.'

'Thank you so much, Mr Sharma.'

'Don't mention it.' Sharma smiled. 'In our profession saying, "you're welcome" isn't taken as something positive. Another piece of advice – do not talk about anything to any person in the lock-up. You never know who's a snitch. Just avoid talking, okay?'

'Yes, sir.' Then: 'Did inspector Arfy tell you what evidence they have against us?'

'No. He doesn't have to tell us anything until he presents it to the court, but I'll find out tonight, don't you worry.'

Sharma looked at his watch; it was almost 5:30 p.m. now, the Hannibal would be at the gate any minute to take Bipin away for the night; it was no longer safe to talk about the case anymore.

Just then, Bhim Singh, the miserable constable with a perpetually foul disposition, entered the room.

'Why do you need to put handcuffs on me?' Bipin asked when he saw them.

'Standard operating procedure,' he responded gruffly, his tone signifying that he was in no mood for debate.

Bipin looked at Sharma who merely nodded. *Yes, it was indeed procedure, nothing more.*

———

Senior Inspector Arfy Khan's budget meeting was with his immediate supervisor, but he had been especially called in by Commissioner Raj Mehra to report on the recent heist and Arfy's progress.

It was a standard request, but for the fact that Mehra abhorred Arfy's guts. He merely needed an excuse to poke Arfy in the gums, which Arfy was well aware of. He knew a verbal whipping was in store for him when he got to the commissioner's office.

'Almost ten bloody hours since you made the arrest of those responsible for the daylight heist, and you have no confession yet?' Mehra barked. 'Are you running an enquiry or a circus, SI Khan?' The commissioner was apoplectic for no apparent reason. Maybe the pressure was getting to him. Ironically, the higher you got up the tree, the shakier the branches were.

It is a circus and we're short of a baboon – want to join? Arfy wanted to say but that would cost him his career, he knew. 'It's complicated, sir; we need to find where the money is hidden first. And after the recent scandal of police atrocities, I thought it would be wise to use a different tactic ...'

'You and your idiotic tactics ... whoever selected you for the police. I don't care what you do, I want the case closed before the weekend. Do you understand?'

'Yes, sir.'

'Now leave. Don't waste my time and your time standing here.'

So much for courtesy!

'Have a good evening, sir.'

———

There were no single-occupancy cells in the police station. Or they were already taken. Bhim Singh marched Bipin to a cell already occupied by three dishevelled, drunk men.

'But ... I'm supposed to be all by myself ...' Bipin protested.

'So who's asking you to cuddle them? Just sleep on your blanket and you'll be on your own.' Bhim Singh took his cuffs off, and, giving him a stern push into the cell, locked it shut. 'Food will be served at eight.'

Either that clown of an inspector had lied to Sharma outright or the sly lawyer had been duplicitous in conveying the message to Bipin. The result was the same, and Sharma was not around to settle the issue. The night would be far more insidious than he had prepared himself for.

The three men in the cell appeared to be drunk out of their wits. But they could still come around to their senses at night and attack him. The stench of alcohol and stale tobacco permeated the closed space. Bipin looked around. The paint on the walls was peeling in several places, and there were dark stains where previous prisoners had sat with their oily heads against the walls. Disgusted beyond words, he decided to stand close to the edge and look out through the iron rods. For the first time in his life, he understood why it was called being behind bars.

Dinner arrived at eight. Tasteless *daal* – which was mostly yellow water – and rice that hadn't been fully boiled. Maybe it was from some dhaba nearby that specialized in *al dente*. Bipin was surprised he could still smile in the face of the events that had occurred since the morning.

The lights were switched off at nine. In place of a bed he was given a threadbare blanket that had definitely been used by previous occupants of this generous spa since, perhaps, before Bipin's birth. One blanket – he could use it as a sheet to cover the dusty floor or actually use it as a blanket. Or roll it up and use it as a pillow; he was spoilt for choice. In the end he decided to spread it on the floor and lie down.

Bipin felt a bit relieved when a night-duty police guard walked in and took a seat in the corridor. He was a true *mushtanda* – a monster, maybe six-foot-six – he could possibly put at least ten men of Bipin's size in a coma with one of his hands.

Relief from imminent physical harm aside, sleep was still elusive with everything that had been going on since morning. His thoughts wandered off.

How had the police investigated and apprehended them in merely three days? He was also worried about the stolen loot lying in the safe house. With both Anuj and he arrested, what would happen to the cash? Okay, the landlord had been paid three-months' rent in advance. But he could still visit the house. Finding neither of the tenants there, he might get curious and open the house with his set of keys. What then? Of course, this was all conjecture. Why should the landlord even bother? However, there was always a chance that the neighbours – not seeing any activity – might report the matter to the landlord or worse still, the police? In any event, what if Sharma and Anuj's lawyer couldn't get them out? A court case would follow and, if they weren't granted bail, in three months they'd lose all the money. Once the police would locate the house, they'd find enough evidence to convict the two accused. Their bags and clothes that were still there would clearly identify them. It would be the end of their stupid and ambitious dream. What were they thinking? They'd be convicted, sent to Tihar Jail and raped or murdered by some violent gang member. Even if they came out alive and unscathed, what would their future be like? As convicted felons – even their parents would disown them; forget about ever securing another job.

Shit! Shit! Shit!

But if all went well, they would be rich. Filthy, fiendishly, flipping rich. They could go anywhere, do anything, live wherever. Life would be so much better if all the dreams Anuj and he had discussed were to come true. They could finally enjoy all the luxuries they had coveted their entire lives. At last, they'd be on an equal footing as those rich brats they'd watched enviously in college. Those attention-seeking bastards who believed their mother's milk was chocolate or strawberry flavoured.

But they had to avoid conviction first. It was, in a way, a paradox. He could have traded one for the other. If he were to be let go, Bipin would happily return the cash and never look back. But giving back the money meant providing the police with an iron-clad case against them. If only they could get out, even on bail. They had passports; they'd hire a car, cross the border into Nepal with the cash somehow, get the currency exchanged before disappearing forever. So close, and yet … However exciting the prospect of an extravagant future was, he had to focus on other things for now.

When sleep gave him a wide berth even at midnight, he couldn't help but ponder. It had been a perfect plan, followed by a pluperfect execution. Where had it all gone wrong?

12

FREE BIRDS

'HOW WAS YOUR FIRST DAY?' BIPIN ASKED ANUJ WHEN HE returned from work.

'Great – I love the job already.'

'What are your responsibilities?'

'Munna ji asked one of the guys to show me how to change the tyres. And since I am not good at anything else, the main part of my job will be to pick up and drop cars at the customers' residence or office.'

'But do you even have a driving licence?'

'We've already applied for it. Munna ji has connections, so I'll have a learner's licence tomorrow, and a permanent one within a week or so.'

'That's impressive.'

'And I get paid every week, in cash. Munna ji doesn't believe in holding his employees' money back until the end of the month.'

'I'm so happy for us,' Manasi chipped in.

'I've promised Manasi I will save so we can go for a proper honeymoon somewhere.'

'Singapore, he's assured me. In fact Anuj and I discussed that since the three of us anyway live together, you should come too, Bipin; it will be fun.'

'What will I do on your honeymoon? I'll be a *kebab mein haddi* ...'

'Of course not.'

'But you guys don't even have passports. You need one to travel—'

'We know that, my friend, and we shall apply for one as soon as we have some money.'

'Can Munna ji help expedite that too?'

'I haven't asked, but he might have connections at the passport office too. All you need is someone, just one person in the particular office who resides in the vicinity and gets their car repaired at our garage. Most customers have been coming to the garage for years now, and they all trust Munna ji, so once he vouches for me, everything can be fast-forwarded in any office.'

'Damn good! I already have a driving licence, why don't you get me a passport too please?'

'It goes without saying, my friend, no trouble at all. We'll all apply for passports together.'

Dinner was a delicious affair with butter paneer masala. Over dinner, Manasi told them she had made the paneer from the milk at home too.

'Amazing.'

'This is delicious, Manasi.'

Misfortune stuck to some people like a bad penny. Anuj
Shastri didn't have a single malicious bone in his body. He
was hot-headed by temperament but never nasty. Indeed,
he had been very careless in life, even a bit arrogant,
closed his mind to taking up a low-paying yet appropriate
job, just to avoid a conventional albeit bourgeois life like
Bipin's or his own father's. And he had always despised
being middle class, yearning to be someone else and do
something grand. But as time passed by, his misguided
ambition had almost ruined his life. He grasped that later
rather than sooner, and regretted losing valuable time in
his lust for an ideal life. Then he'd fallen in love – nothing
wrong with that either; more than half the world fell in
love at some point in their lives – which, for no apparent
reason but that he didn't have a job, irked his father so
much he had thrown his son out of the house. But Bipin
could sense his friend was turning the corner now. Anuj
had understood he had to shoulder the responsibility of
Manasi and their unborn child, and he finally awakened
to face reality. He didn't start as the president or CEO of a
Fortune 500, but everyone had to start somewhere. Bipin
appreciated that his friend had swallowed his pride in a bid
to be more responsible.

Unfortunately, fate had other plans.

One afternoon, after only two weeks of Anuj working at Munna ji's garage, Bipin received a call while he was at work. It was Manasi, and she was howling uncontrollably.

'What happened, Manasi? What's wrong?'

In staccato words, in-between breaking down and wheezing, Manasi mumbled that Anuj had had a serious accident at work. 'Munna ji … has taken … taken him … he's at a private clinic … he's unconscious. Blood … blood. Come here, Bipin …'

'Come where? Munna ji's garage?' Sensing Manasi's impaired state of mind, Bipin felt his own pulse rising. 'What has happened? Where are you right now?'

Fortunately, someone else from Munna ji's garage took the phone from her and gave Bipin the address where they had taken Anuj.

'Thanks. I'll leave now. I should be there in thirty minutes.'

Bipin told his boss he had a family emergency and ran out of the office. Later, he would remember those as the most excruciating thirty minutes of his life. Dear god! He hailed the nearest autorickshaw and jumped into it.

'Where to, *sahib*?'

'Mehta Clinic, GK I, and as quickly as you can, please.'

The clinic was, in a nutshell, a dump. But it was close to Munna ji's garage where the accident had occurred and they had dispatched an ambulance immediately to pick Anuj up. That, and the owner of the clinic, Dr Raj K. Mehta was a long-term client of Munna ji, who helped expedite the process.

When Bipin arrived after exactly thirty minutes – thanks to an excellent autorickshaw driver – Manasi was half lucid, half frantic. This was not surprising, considering her husband, the father of their unborn child, was presumably fighting for his life. It was evident she would cry till she ran out of tears, which wouldn't be anytime soon.

Munna ji, standing beside Manasi and consoling her, stepped forward, shook hands with Bipin and introduced himself. He was over six feet, with the body of a retired wrestler. Bipin estimated his age at near fifty. He wore jeans, rolled up, no socks and denim sneakers and a greyish polo t-shirt with so many grease stains it was difficult to tell its original colour. Given the tense situation, no pleasantries were exchanged and, after the brisk hellos, Munna ji narrated the incident that had taken place back at his garage. Anuj had been changing a wheel this morning when the jack, on which the car was precariously balanced, slipped. It seemed that the rookie apprentice hadn't double-checked if the jack was firmly in place – he had missed the crucial step of securing a fastener after the device was elevated to the desired height; maybe he overlooked it, or maybe he didn't remember before he removed both the wheels on the driver's side. The jack gave way, and the car had come crashing down with his right hand under it. Anuj had fallen unconscious and lost a lot of blood. As the other mechanics rushed to pull him out from under the car, Munna ji had called Dr Mehta who dropped everything else to attend to Anuj.

'We had to bring Anuj to the closest clinic to save him,' Munna ji told Bipin and glanced at Manasi. 'I don't think she's eaten anything since morning, and given her condition, I think you should ask her to eat something please.' His sheer stature might have been daunting but his politeness belied his size.

Bipin nodded. He could see Munna ji's point. 'Is Anuj still in danger?'

'No. Dr Mehta has his best team in the theatre. He came out for a few minutes to tell me Anuj is out of danger. They're operating on his right hand, sewing it up since there was a deep gash. They are also checking for any fractures ...'

'How much longer will it be?'

'Dr Mehta should be out in another fifteen minutes, don't worry. Just talk to Manasi. I think she'll only calm down if you explain it to her.'

Convincing Manasi wasn't easy. She had insisted on seeing Anuj before she ate anything, so they waited.

Dr Mehta came out after twenty-five minutes and walked directly towards Munna ji, who waved to Bipin to join them.

'He's unconscious right now due to the anaesthesia. He is out of any danger, but we will need to keep him under observation for a few days.'

'Thank god,' Munna ji said. 'He's part of my family, Dr Mehta, so please do not worry about expenses—'

'Oh, please, you don't even have to mention that, Munna ji.'

'His hand …' Bipin asked tentatively, 'will it be alright?'

Dr Mehta hesitated a little. 'He has no fractures in his wrist, thankfully. He narrowly escaped a permanent injury, but sadly, we had to amputate his ring finger.'

'Dear god!' Bipin uttered under his breath, he didn't want Manasi to hear this. Not yet. He reckoned she should see Anuj first before they broke the news of a missing digit in his right hand.

'But given that the car had fallen straight on his hand … how heavy would the car have been, Munna ji? About nine hundred to a thousand kilos?'

'About that, yes.'

'A thousand kilograms could have crushed the entire hand. Like I said he is lucky we managed to save his entire hand except one finger. He'd already lost a lot of blood. If there had been any delay, it could have been difficult to save the hand itself,' he smiled.

Munna ji and Bipin returned watery smiles. The doctor had done his best. Anuj would live. In the grand scheme of things how important was one finger in the universe? But for the person who'd lost one from a hand it would mean quite be a lot.

'He will be in Intensive Care tonight and so I request you all to just see him through the glass since we do not want him to catch any infection. Once he is conscious, one of you can meet him for a few minutes. He should be fine and lucid by tomorrow.'

'How long before we can take him home?' Bipin asked.

'Two to three days. Of course, he will need to return for regular check-ups from time to time.'

'Thank you, Dr Mehta,' Munna ji said.

'Thank you.'

'You're welcome,' Dr Mehta said and left them to see other patients.

Manasi didn't know about Anuj's missing finger when she saw him in the ICU. Anuj, too, was unaware since his entire hand was under layers of bandages. The doctor had warned that up to eighty percent of the individuals with any kind of amputation experienced phantom sensations in their amputated part – in Anuj's case the ring finger – and those sensations were always painful. So while recovering from the surgery, Anuj would not realize his finger had been amputated; it seemed best to keep it that way until the bandages could be taken off.

After a lot of cajoling, Bipin persuaded Manasi to go home and rest because no one was permitted to stay with Anuj in the ICU.

Bipin took a leave of absence and both Manasi and he were back to see him in the morning. Anuj was conscious;

he had been on fluids until late last night, but had been given sandwiches later. He was pleased to see his wife and his friend. The strong painkillers had numbed the pain, and the bandage concealed the secret well. Munna ji dropped by in the afternoon to see his protégé. He reiterated that the entire hospitalization bill would be taken care of by him. Munna ji also told Anuj to take time off, rest and that he would not stop his weekly allowance.

'You have already done so much, Munna ji.'

'It was an accident at work, and I feel I'm just as responsible, so it's not for you to decide. It's my decision, okay?' Munna ji ended the debate.

In any event, why was Anuj even trying to strangle an inward flow of money? Bipin wondered.

'I told you he is a generous man,' Anuj told Manasi and Bipin after his boss had left.

'It's incredible – I mean you've only been working there for a week or two; he could have easily washed his hands of you after sending you to the doctor.'

'He could have, but he didn't; he takes care of his people.'

———

Dr Mehta's assessment had been correct. A week later, when the news that his finger had been amputated to save him was given to Anuj and Manasi, it was less of a shock then than it would have been if it were made known upfront while Anuj was in a fragile state. He complained of phantom pains off and on, but was able to cope with it well. Anuj even joked that because Manasi hadn't given him a wedding band, he had done away with his ring finger.

Two weeks after the accident and surgery, only suture marks and the cast on his fingers remained, and he started going to work. Munna ji gave him a desk job this time round, to look after the cash and accounts until he recovered fully. Nothing that should cause any physical distress.

Although losing any part of one's body can be quite traumatic, a missing ring finger did not prove too much of a hindrance in carrying on a normal life. But whenever the three of them sat together and Anuj looked at the stump of his missing finger, he became despondent.

'It was my ring finger.'

'But we never exchanged rings at our wedding,' Manasi reminded him.

'That's because we couldn't afford to buy them, my sweetheart wife. If it hadn't been for the generosity of Bipin's dad, we didn't even have the money for the simple wedding we had.'

'Look at this way, Anuj – you have a wife and no finger, and I have a finger and no wife. Which one would you rather have?'

'That's a good point,' Manasi agreed with Bipin; anything to soften the hurt.

'I guess you guys are right. Also, it will be less expensive when we can finally afford a ring.'

How? Both of them wanted to ask but didn't.

'We'll only need to buy one for Manasi so we'll buy a real big diamond one. And for my phantom finger, a phantom ring will do.' He laughed at his own joke.

'That's more like my husband.'

———

Barring the visual shock, the wound healed well and fast. By the end of a little over three weeks, Anuj was as good as before except for some pain. The scar tissue hurt sometimes, but he was eager to prove to Manasi he was man enough to bear pain rather than admit he was hurting. And he succeeded. He had insisted that *his* parents should never be informed about the accident. He was adamant he didn't want them to accept him because of any sort of sympathy. If they cared for their son they'd come to him regardless of his status or illness.

However, it had been almost a month since Bipin's father had started his dialogue with Manasi's parents. It's difficult to tell if one gets wiser as one ages but the older one gets, the better you get at handling complex situations; Mr Desai had a strong inclination it would be far easier to convince Manasi's parents than the Shastris. Mr Shastri was way more obstinate than Mr Upadhaya. Moreover, with Manasi expecting a child, persuading Manasi's mother would be simpler too. Maybe, once he had convinced them, the Shastri family might give in too, but he wasn't holding his breath. And he hadn't been off the mark.

Mr and Mrs Desai's first visit had been met with reticence, a reserved hostility. They weren't thrown out, but it had been made amply clear that the Desais weren't welcome. Certainly not after they had been instrumental in getting their daughter married to the wayward good-for-nothing Anuj. Mr Upadhaya, in a roundabout way, had told them that meddling in someone else's affairs didn't suit a respectable couple.

But the seed had been sown. Mrs Upadhaya's heart started to thaw. A week later, she had called upon Mrs Desai to ask if she was in touch with *them*. The next week she wanted to send a hello, then love, then blessings.

Long story short, when the news of Anuj's accident reached Mrs Upadhaya, she decided enough was enough. With Anuj recuperating from surgery, who would look after her pregnant daughter? Didn't she, as a mother, owe that to her child? She told her husband she wanted to see her daughter with an ultimatum: 'She's my daughter, and she needs me at this moment. If I don't help her, who will? And, God forbid, if something untoward happened to her child, she would never forgive us. Do you want to face the lord's wrath that you deserted your daughter when she needed you most?'

'*Hare Krishna*, you're right. We must visit them.'

And thus followed the first family reunion. Manasi was happy to see her parents, and so was Anuj. Manasi's mother was glad that the three friends stayed together, but she was also sceptical if this was the right arrangement for her daughter in the circumstances. *She'll need help and advice from time to time. Also, medical check-ups. Moreover, she too had gone to her mother when she was expecting Manasi so there was no reason why Manasi shouldn't come back to her mother ... It seemed logical to Mrs Upadhaya.*

She presented valid arguments, and in the end Manasi and Anuj relented. They agreed that Anuj would drop Manasi off at her parents' place in a week so that she could rest – after all she had already been through a lot because of Anuj's accident. But it was best to leave the past behind.

Anuj kept his promise. The following week, after the three friends filled in their passport applications, he borrowed a car from Munna ji and he and Bipin dropped Manasi off at her parents' home for a brief sojourn.

DAY TWO

FRIDAY, 17 JANUARY 1997
SADAR POLICE STATION
GURGAON, HARYANA

13

JAILBIRDS

BIPIN WOKE UP TO STRANGE NOISES IN THE BACKGROUND. He hadn't expected to fall asleep but sometime after three in the morning, his tired body had given up and he had slipped under the blanket of sleep. It was probably for the best because he presumably had another long day ahead of him. Inspector Arfy Khan didn't look like someone who'd give anyone a free pass. He hoped and prayed that Mr Sharma had been able to procure the information he was charging them for. One lakh ... it was a fucking rip-off!

There was only one toilet-cum-bathroom at the end of the corridor that served the four-or-five holding cells in the police station. One had to queue up to get into the stinking stall. Bipin wondered if he might see Anuj in the queue but Arfy seemed to have foreseen this scenario and planned accordingly. Maybe Anuj had been held somewhere else overnight; no wonder the miserable-looking constable

Bhim Singh who had brought Bipin here had taken much longer when he had gone to drop Anuj.

Bummer!

There was no bolt on the door on the inside. Every individual had a ten-minute quota and once your turn arrived and you got into the bathroom, if you weren't out in that time, the guard on duty had the right to barge in and drag you out. It didn't matter if you were constipated and had a turd hanging out of your bottom. The guard had sniggered when he had outlined the rule to the other detainees. Ten minutes meant exactly ten minutes by *his* watch.

Once in the bathroom, Bipin realized that a shower or bath was out of question. The stall wasn't equipped for it. There was a tap, but no bucket. In any event, there were no towels to dry oneself, even if one decided to sit under the tap. A stainless-steel sink had been bolted onto the wall; it didn't look like it had been cleaned anytime in the last year. There was an almost completely squished-out tube of Colgate and getting anything out of the damn thing was like pulling teeth. There were no toothbrushes around, and Bipin knew the guard wasn't dispensing any toiletries so he used his finger to rub his teeth with whatever little toothpaste he could squeeze out. It was more to refresh his breath than any cleaning it would provide. He looked up at the broken mirror above the sink, and saw that his eyes were bloodshot and he had developed dark circles under his eyes, clearly due to lack of sleep and fatigue. He took some water and washed his face. Taking some in his hand he ran his fingers through his hair. With that, he hurried out.

'Good boy, nine minutes,' applauded the guard. 'Next one in. You know the rules.'

———

Tea was served with two soggy rusks, which made Bipin wonder if they had been stored in some damp basement only to frustrate the prisoners.

Bhim Singh – as foul-faced as the previous day – came to escort Bipin to the office at nine. Singh handcuffed Bipin before taking him out of the block and marching him into the office. As they reached SI Arfy Khan's office, he declared, 'I've brought both of them in now.'

'Thank you, Bhim Singh, take him to the same room he was in yesterday,' Arfy told him and then looked at Bipin, 'I'll see you first, I need to talk to your lawyer regarding something important.'

The room was humid and sticky. Maybe it had rained the night before. Perhaps the rusks had got wet in the rain. Anyway, it also felt a lot cooler, which was better than the previous day when the heat had been cranked up to roast him.

Bipin was lost in humdrum thoughts when Advocate Sharma walked inside. 'Good morning. How was your night?'

'I had to share a cell with three other men, so I could hardly sleep.'

'You should have called me immediately.'

'Like I had a choice,' Bipin sighed in exasperation. There were bigger battles to fight than bickering over last night. 'Anyway, did you manage to contact Anuj's lawyer?'

'Well, the good news is the culpable-homicide charges that the inspector frightened us about yesterday are no longer applicable. The man, whom one of you had *presumably* accidentally hurt has been released from the hospital, so all good on that front. That was my primary concern, since a manslaughter charge is very serious, which I'm sure you understand.'

'Yes, sir.'

Sharma sat down with a finger against his chin to demonstrate – what could be, only to him – an impression that he was deep in thought. 'Regarding the other thing—'

The door flung open without any warning and SI Arfy Khan plummeted in. To save face, he turned around to see what exactly he had tripped on this time but found no evidence except his own clumsiness.

'Good morning, gentlemen. I hope you had a wonderful stay in the lock-up last night, Mr Bantu Desai? He smiled at Bipin sarcastically.

It's BIPIN, you bloody idiot!

'It was adequate, sir, I survived,' Bipin responded politely.

'That's the spirit, sonny boy. Now ...' he turned to Sharma. 'Hello, Mr Sherlock Holmes or should I call you

James Bond? Actually neither of the two names fit you since you failed in your secret mission, didn't you?' Arfy passed another mocking smile that made Sharma flush red. Shame? Guilt of being caught out?

'I'm not sure what you are talking about, Mr Khan.'

'Senior Inspector Arfy Khan. Mister is used for civilians, Mr Sharma.'

'I'm sorry.'

'You should be, not for this, but for trying to obstruct the course of an active police investigation. You asked one of your despicable contacts to seek privileged and classified information from one of the junior officers in my department—'

'Of course not, I wouldn't do anything like that.'

'Yes, of course, you wouldn't do such a thing. You would farm out the task to someone who cannot be linked back to you.'

'This is defamation, Senior Inspector Khan.' Sharma couldn't even persuade his own face to believe it, but as Arfy had already mentioned: he couldn't prove it either.

Bipin felt a sense of emptiness watching the two engage in a verbal duel. But, at least, Sharma had tried digging up the information for which he was charging Bipin a large sum of money. The money was actually being spent and not going into Sharma's pocket – although, Arfy's comments made it amply clear Sharma's efforts had not been successful.

The argument was in the third person after it was established that *someone's* attempt at bribing an officer of the law had been futile. Both Arfy and Sharma knew who that someone was, but in the absence of any evidence Arfy thought it best to make veiled threats. Sharma would try again, given an opportunity, but he would probably ask his contacts to be more discreet. Bribes had been paid before, they would be offered again. It wasn't as if no policeman had ever accepted a backhander. However, the bickering continued until Arfy and Sharma both declared that whoever had attempted such a despicable act should be punished. Eventually, the inspector and the advocate were on the same team, both deploring the move. Ridiculous!

'Why would you want to get in touch with Anuj's lawyer anyway? What would she or he tell you differently when I am already communicating between the two of you?'

That is *the problem,* Bipin thought. Like Sharma had forewarned him, Arfy was playing them against each other.

'I wouldn't and I didn't.' Sharma, after the initial shame of getting caught out had dissolved, spoke confidently.

'If you say so, sure.' Arfy shrugged disbelievingly.

'So, the manslaughter charge is off since we know the injured person was in a stable enough condition to walk out of the hospital on his own.' Sharma, decided to segue into the case.

Thank god. Bipin closed his eyes for a second.

'Yes, that is true.'

'May I know what other evidence you have against my client to charge him?'

'I don't have to provide you with the evidence, and you know that. But let me think. Maybe if I show the evidence to you and sonny boy here, it might jog his sleeping memory.'

'So what is this evidence, sir?' Bipin asked.

'Where's the cash, sonny boy?'

'Don't say anything, Bipin,' warned Sharma.

'Give me an hour. Your learned friend – isn't that how lawyers address each other in courtrooms? – also attempted the same feat last night.' Arfy stopped and smiled, waiting for Sharma to contradict him again, but Sharma stayed calm. 'Let me also tell you that your learned friend, Anuj's lawyer's attempt was also unsuccessful.' Arfy clapped his hands and let out a derisive laugh.

Sharma and Bipin didn't say anything, and just glanced at each other.

'Oh, yeah, he wanted to find you and you wanted to find her or him. But unfortunately, both of you failed. Do you know why?'

Sharma didn't take the bait. He knew Arfy would gloat anyway.

'Because you were up against a brilliant opponent, that's why: yours truly, Senior Inspector Arfy Khan.'

God, this clown is so full of himself, Bipin thought.

'I might appear like Winnie the Pooh but all said and done, you must not forget that the role of Winnie is, after all, played by a bear.'

Surprised looks again. Bipin looked at Sharma to see if he had any clue where this discussion was headed.

Arfy carried on regardless. 'You know which is the only land animal that can fight the apex predator, the African lion? The brown bear can finish a lion – the so-called king of the jungle, within minutes. It can completely demolish a lion. It's fortunate for the lion that he and the brown bear have different habitats. My advice to you both is: don't ever test the strength of a bear. I might look like a cuddly teddy, but I am not.' With that warning scraped from the Discovery Channel, Arfy Khan stood up, and without toppling forward or backward, marched out of the room.

———

'What now?' asked Bipin after he waited a few moments. He had seen the red light on the camera was off; he didn't require Sharma to remind him every time.

'I don't know. You just saw the pasting I got from that inspector for going out on a limb for you.'

'But it was your idea to begin with, wasn't it?'

'It was, but I only suggested it for your benefit. And it boomeranged. I've never been insulted like this, ever.'

And I bet you've never been paid five lakh rupees for a case either. 'I can only apologize, Mr Sharma, but what's happened has happened. We need to think ahead.'

'How certain are you that your friend ... Anuj, will not sell you out?'

'He wouldn't.' Bipin didn't need to think.

'No matter what the price?'

'No matter whatever the price,' Bipin reiterated; he had absolute confidence in his friend.

'Not even in exchange for a lesser sentence? Not for money, not for freedom?'

'I told you, nothing can turn Anuj against me.' Bipin was resolute.

'And how confident are you that he has the same confidence in you?'

'What do you mean?'

'Arfy will try his tactics on both of you. You sound assured that whatever Arfy tells you, you won't believe it since you have unwavering trust in your friend, right?'

'Yes.'

'But when – not if – when Anuj is told that you are ready to abandon him for a lesser sentence or money or whatever, would he have the same trust in you? Would he be as certain that you would not betray him at any cost?'

'Of course, he won't believe Arfy,' Bipin was assertive.

'I can only hope you're right. I pray for your sake that Anuj doesn't desert you, saying it was your idea ...'

'No way.'

'OK, I'll just sneak out for a quick smoke break.'

———

Sharma walked out to see Constable Bhim Singh whispering something to SI Khan. Conscious of Sharma's sudden presence outside the interrogation room, Arfy looked at him, then turned to the constable and told him sternly – the warning was meant as much for the constable as for Sharma. 'None of the four – the suspects or their lawyers – should be permitted into the toilet in succession; after any of them visits it, I want you to go in and search. Then get them cleaned. Toilets are notorious places for hiding notes – these guys must have done it all through their college lives,' he looked admonishingly at Sharma, like he was daring the advocate to challenge him.

SI Arfy Khan seemed to be determined to devise the most unassailable barriers to prevent any contamination of testimonies. Even better than some of the courtrooms that Sharma had been in. He remained mute and expressionless. After all, it was the inspector's right to impede any interaction between the two suspects.

'I don't care if they wet their pants … or panties, but they have to wait until the toilets have been cleaned and checked.'

Sharma didn't challenge that either. However, the mention of panties rankled him once again. Was Arfy trying to tell him something? Was Anuj's lawyer a woman? How had his contacts missed it in the overnight search despite the promise of the hefty payment? If only he had another day, when he got out this evening, he would order a targeted manhunt … no, a womanhunt. But the inspector wasn't going to permit that, he knew. Knowing whether Anuj's lawyer was a woman or a man would be pointless by tomorrow.

14

FREE BIRDS

IF ANYONE WERE TO ASK WHOSE IDEA IT WAS, IT WAS *theirs*. Neither could point at the other, and neither could escape or blame the other for having persuaded or cajoled or arm-twisted. It was a joint idea, a shared plan. *Who* proposed it was irrelevant. *Who* put more time into planning was immaterial. They were in it together; they both wanted the money equally. Thankfully, if there were any guarantees in life it was that neither Bipin nor Anuj would ever throw the other under a bus. They'd rather sacrifice themselves. It wasn't just friendship. Like Anuj and Manasi had once said, they were a family, a unit.

When Manasi had left the two to go to her mother's place, she provided all the victuals the two guys required, except alcohol. Hence, after dropping Manasi at her parents' place, the boys had returned home after picking up a bottle of Old Monk, several bottles of cola and finger food on the way. It had been a while since they'd spent time in just each other's company. Sometimes, during their college days, Bipin and Anuj used to get together on the roof of the DDA flats in Munirka and drink into the night, the stars shining down on them. Back then, with most of their lives ahead of them, they had so much to dream about. Reality hadn't sunk in. At the time, it used to be a hush-hush affair, as they had to be careful that the parents – or the nosey neighbours – didn't get a whiff of their drunken escapades. But now, they didn't have a care in the world. They had exclusive rights to the terrace and the barsaati; it was their lair with no possibility of intervention from any neighbours or parents as long as they didn't create a ruckus. They were independent adults.

Two drinks down, the anguish of broken dreams and unrealized aspirations swept over the discussions. The way they were progressing in their lives and careers, the visions they had had in college about their future seemed like delusions more than achievable targets. It felt like they were chasing mirages.

'We're like street dogs chasing cars …'

'How did we end up like this?' Anuj asked, and justifiably so. His earnings were meagre, he had a pregnant wife, and he lived in a friend's one-room barsaati. If it weren't for Bipin he wouldn't be able to make ends meet. He'd be out on the streets.

'Why do you say that?' Bipin stayed calm for his friend.

'I mean, what happened to our dreams of doing something substantial, making it big. The way we're living isn't what we had imagined, is it?'

'No, but we don't have much choice. There simply aren't any opportunities. I'm trying for another job—'

'That's not going to change our lives drastically. Another two-or-three thousand rupees a month isn't going to turn your sailboat into a yacht. We need to think big, Bipin.'

'I've spent over five years working at two companies, and I can assure you we were way off the mark when we thought we'd ever be on a par with those rich brats we studied with at college. It was a flight of fantasy, my friend. It's nearly impossible to cross the boundaries of the class divide—'

'What do you mean?' Anuj asked, refilling the glasses with Old Monk. He went to the refrigerator and pulled out a bottle of cola, pouring exactly half into each tumbler. 'We might run out of cola,' he mused. 'Okay, where were we?'

'Like I was saying, people like us who are born into the middle class rarely get opportunities to strike big. We are small fish in a small pond; our area of influence is insignificant – even if you could run a marathon, there isn't enough ground for you to run on. I'll be twenty-seven next year, and I'm still a junior manager, which is no more than a glorified clerk in the private sector to be honest. Many employees who came from better colleges or who had contacts in the industry have already gone up a rung on the ladder. They're being groomed to lead the company and people like me, in the future. There is no career path for me, and this is after I've worked diligently, put in more hours than a lot of them … you see what I mean?' Bipin picked up his glass and took a generous sip. His painful soliloquy on his gloomy future had dried his tongue and moistened his eyes.

'There has to be a way out of this drudgery.'

'Sometimes I think I should have taken a public-sector job like my father had advised. I'd still earn the same amount I'm earning today with significantly less workload and more stability. At my present job, if I make a small mistake or if my new manager doesn't like my face, I'll be shown the door in no time. I'm on tenterhooks all the time, wondering how long I can hold on. And the worst part is – after knowing all this, the motivation is at an all-time low. I just keep my head down and do what I'm told.'

'I always thought you were doing much better than that, I'm sorry to hear that – that's really sad.'

'I know, but like I said before, what other choice do I have?'

Anuj prepared the fourth drink.

'We should probably go slow,' Bipin remarked. 'I think I'm getting drunk, talking more than I should …'

'Who cares? Tomorrow is Sunday, we'll sleep until the afternoon.'

'As a matter of fact, I think you have far better prospects than me.'

'How is that so?'

'Anuj, while I'm a hyped white-collar clerk in the office, you're actually learning a skill. I know your father – and father-in-law – might consider being a mechanic's sidekick a blue-collar worker, but keep that middle-class narrow-

mindedness aside for a moment and think about it ...
Munna ji, today, has more influence than your father and
my father combined. He could call a doctor who rushed
an ambulance to save you. Could our fathers have done
the same? So, you might be a trainee today, but with the
vocational skills you're learning, you could open your own
garage in say, five years' time?'

'Here's to AB garage,' Anuj raised his glass as a toast
and upended it.

'Slow down, my friend, slow down. I have no desire to
clean up if you puke here.' Bipin looked around the terrace.
'And what does AB stand for in your garage by the way?'

'Anuj and Bipin.'

'I'm honoured.'

'But remember when you come to work at AB Garage,
you will have to change tyres to start with.'

'Of course.'

'If it hadn't been for you, brother, I'd be on the streets.'
Anuj, four drinks down, was getting emotional, like all
drunks.

'It's not true. You found a job when we needed it most.
If it hadn't been for me you'd have found one earlier. If
anything, I delayed you. What kind of brother am I?'

Before they knew it, the two were crying, their throats
constricting. Maudlin after four – or was it five? – large
pegs of Old Monk, they promised each other that they
would one day take over the world. They would win it all,
not realizing that if anything, presently it was the alcohol
that was winning.

'One for the road, as they say?' asked Anuj.

'What road … *hic*! We just have to, have to … walk in.'

'No, you wait here, I'll walk in.' Anuj went in to get the colas, but it took him far longer to find the bottle in the refrigerator and then the damn bottle opener. He eventually managed to make the drinks with the leftover cola and water. It tasted strong.

'We have to do something … something out of the … *hic*! … out of the ordinary, my brother Anuj.'

'Yeah, let's rob a bank.'

'Good idea … bloody good idea, brother.'

Anuj raised his right hand to form a finger gun raising his thumb over the fist to look like a hammer, his index finger upright like a barrel, and pressed the trigger with his middle finger. There, raised against the backdrop, the ring finger was conspicuously absent, and a fresh burst of tears flowed down his cheeks.

'Don't cry brother … *hic*! We will … *hic*! make the worl' pay fo thish finger, I … pro-mish.' Bipin knew he was talking gibberish, but he was plastered, and he could think of no other way to calm his equally inebriated friend.

Neither of them knew when sleep took over while they were on the mattresses on the terrace outside.

———

The naked truth was, humans took what they had for granted: it was their birthright. A large majority of people only tended to seek the possessions or positions that they coveted. They coveted things they saw every day. And they only saw what they didn't have. But if all humans were created equal, why was the world divided into haves and have-nots? The haves were blessed, some have-nots got lucky as they moved through life; others waited for their turn, which never came. Anyway, waiting without effort was pointless. You could wait until the end of time and still come up empty-handed. Or ... or? Some believed that the ends surely justified the means and thus the means of acquisition could differ, and consequently there were infinite roads that led to the same destination.

Bipin woke up at four in the morning. The alcohol had caused severe dehydration, his stomach grumbled, the acidic bile rising in his throat. Sick! He was sick to the core. And beside him lay Anuj, asleep but aware of how cruel the world was. Anuj and he had every right to feel dejected. What had they achieved so far? Worse still, like they had discussed the previous night, there were no promises in the future that they could look forward to. Not even the proverbial light at the end of this endless tunnel of drudgery. Even though both their fathers had held on to steady jobs, provided meals on the table, clothes, and paid of their college education, it somehow pinched. Being middle class resembled a curse. Their parents had inadvertently passed the gene on to them, and if the circle didn't break, Manasi and Anuj would pass it to the next generation. So would Bipin, when he got married and had children. Middle class but existing in the working-class circle. The circle ended where it began – that was its DNA. Whoever got out of it without breaking it?

Rob a bank, he smiled inwardly as he got up and rushed to the toilet and retched. He washed his face and went foraging for some biscuits in the kitchenette. On finding some, he devoured them like a starving animal.

It was August, the sun was swelling somewhere on the horizon, its first light had kissed the sky already. Daybreak. Thankfully, it was Sunday, but he felt depressed thinking about the looming week. The same grind would begin again.

Anuj was up too. He looked around and saw Bipin standing at the door of the barsaati looking out, eating something.

'You're up early.'

'You are too.'

'God! I have a headache,' Anuj said as he lazily got up and walked in.

'Have some biscuits and pop an aspirin. I've just had one.'

'I feel yuck.'

'I told you to go slow, didn't I?' Bipin reminded him of the sage advice he had dispensed, but they had still carried on drinking.

'Yes, you did, but it was too much fun to stop.'

'Also too many sorrows to drown,' Bipin prompted.

'Yes, yes, and of course, we even planned to rob a bank.'

The second time around, the phrase 'rob a bank' didn't sound as weird or awkward. It seemed to have lost the bite.

'Seriously?' Bipin asked, despite the memory that had popped up just moments before Anuj had woken up.

'You don't remember?'

'Now that you mention it, I do have a vague memory of it. Did we actually make a plan?

'Are you crazy?'

'Coffee?'

'Oh, yes. Need caffeine.'

'Or hair of the dog?'

'Do you really mean that?'

'Certainly, why not? We have Old Monk left,' Bipin pointed at the bottle which still lay on the terrace outside beside the mattresses they had slept on. The glasses were there too, with some dark liquid still remaining at the bottom. 'We have a bottle of cola that I couldn't find last night, and it's Sunday, so we can indulge if we want to.'

'Then we go rob a bank,' Anuj mocked.

The third time 'rob a bank' was mentioned, it sounded banal.

The fourth time 'rob a bank' was vented after the two raised their glasses and said *cheers* with their hair of the dog, and it resonated like an option.

The fifth time it felt like a real possibility, which was maybe worth considering.

The sixth time, the *maybe* was dropped.

They quickly finished their first drink of the morning and gave it serious thought.

15

JAILBIRDS

ROUGHLY AN HOUR AFTER LEAVING THEM IN THE interrogation room, Senior Inspector Arfy Khan returned with a sly smile on his face. He sat down with the file in front of him. Bipin wondered what was in the box-file that he had been carrying around for the past twenty-four hours, and in all that time he had opened it but once to confirm Anuj's name when he had wrongly called him Atul or Alok and Bipin had corrected him.

'I have to say, Mr Sharma, that your counterpart, the other sonny boy's lawyer, did a better job than you – they came close to identifying you,' Arfy opened his mouth after he settled in his chair without falling off.

'Then why didn't he contact me?'

'What makes you so sure it's a *he*?

'Is it a lady advocate then?'

'He, she, it, them, they … why does it matter? The sad part is they've only come into *some* knowledge – and I'm not sure they were able to precisely identify you. They know it's a Mr Sharma, but they don't know the first name and finding an advocate by the name of Sharma in Delhi is like searching for the proverbial needle. So, I'd say they'll need to call a hundred Sharmas before they get to you.'

So that was the reason for the crafty smile on the silly face.

'So, Mr Bhola Desai, what have you thought about our little discussion? Do you remember anything about the robbery between Noida and Delhi?'

Bipin, you effing moron!

'Don't say anything,' Sharma warned.

'Your choice,' said Arfy, before putting his hand in his trouser pocket as though he had a severe itch in his gonads, but instead pulled out a card and put it on the small table for both Sharma and Bipin to see. 'We found this at the scene of the crime.'

'This is Anuj's driving licence,' Bipin said without picking up the card.

'Aren't you the master of the obvious, sonny boy? It says Anuj Shastri, it even has his picture on the card. Even Advocate Sharma can see what this damn little piece of plastic is.'

'Why are you carrying it?' Bipin asked straight-faced. This was the only slip-up, the only thing he had dreaded.

'I just told you that it was found at the scene of the crime, in the van that you know nothing about.'

'I indeed don't know anything about the van, you're right.'

'Your friend tells me that you had borrowed his driving licence a few weeks back and hadn't returned it to him yet, which puts you, and not him, at the crime scene.'

'That's bullshit.'

'Watch your language, sonny boy. That kind of language isn't acceptable when you're talking to me. If you were my kid, I'd have slapped you across the face so hard its marks would remain for weeks, not days.'

Sharma realized that Arfy had craftily worded the warning again. *If you were my kid …* was a hypothetical situation. No judge would accept that as a legit threat.

'I'm sorry, sir.'

'Good boy. Apology accepted. Now, tell me why did you borrow or steal your friend's driving licence?'

Bipin remained quiet. He knew how the inspector had found the licence. He didn't want to utter anything and implicate Anuj or himself.

'Mr Sharma, I think I might have a few other charges against your client here. IPC Section 416 for impersonating someone else. Also, using someone else's government-issued ID is deemed perjury under IPC Section 193, isn't it? So should we remove the manslaughter charges and include these two?' Arfy looked at Bipin. A soft threat.

'There has to be some mistake, I never borrowed Anuj's driving licence …'

'Very strange. Why would your friend lie to me on record then?'

'Bipin, stop talking,' Sharma called out. If Bipin kept talking, it was only a matter of time before he'd lose it and come up with some allegation to counter his friend's claim when it was apparent that Arfy was lying blatantly. He was practising the theory of prisoner's dilemma to the hilt – twisting and turning and fine-tuning the statements to suit his need.

Arfy waited a minute, but realized that Bipin had taken his advocate's advice; he wasn't talking anymore.

'Okay, could someone solve this mystery for me, please? If you weren't carrying your friend's licence, and he didn't have it since he had loaned it to you, how did a driving licence get into a van on its own? Can a driving licence drive itself?' Arfy laughed like he had cracked another smart one.

Neither Bipin nor Sharma responded.

Then, suddenly, an idea sparked in Bipin's mind. He hadn't seen Anuj anywhere in this place since yesterday. Neither here nor in the holding cells or whatever the police called that stinking cell he had been locked in overnight. Maybe Anuj wasn't in this police station at all. Maybe Arfy was only giving them second-hand info that someone else was feeding him from another place. If Arfy wasn't directly in touch with Anuj who knew what else this crooked inspector was lying about?

'Anuj isn't here, he's not in this police station,' he blurted out without thinking or consulting Mr Sharma.

'What piece of information made you deduce that claptrap, sonny boy?'

'I didn't see him last night or this morning. If he's in the same jail shouldn't I have?'

'I haven't seen God. That does not mean He doesn't exist.'

'That's not the answer to my question.'

'I don't have to answer any of your silly questions, sonny boy. I ask the questions, you decide whether you want to answer them here or in court tomorrow ...' Arfy looked at Sharma, '... or do whatever your lawyer uncle tells you to do. I'm only trying to help you here. But it's quite strange that you should say that your friend Anil Shastri isn't here when I just shook hands with him before coming here. For your kind information, we are this close ...' Arfy raised his right hand and held his thumb and index finger an inch apart to emphasize '... to closing out a deal.' The cunning smile appeared on his lips again.

'You shook hands with Anuj?'

'Didn't I just say that? Yes, I said that. Why can't I shake hands with Mr Ajit Shastri ji? Is he the Pope or the president of Timbuktu? Or is he a shy kind of homophobic guy who doesn't shake hands with other men?'

'I didn't mean that, sir.'

'Oh, so you are surprised I shook hands with a criminal. But that's how one seals a deal, isn't it?'

'That's clear, sir. Did you notice his wedding band, sir?'

'Should I have?'

'Do you know what kind of wedding band Anuj wears?'
Bipin knew the truth would be out in a minute – this
would confirm if Anuj was around and if Arfy had actually
met him.

'Is this a test I'm supposed to take for you?'

'No, sir, I was just asking you that if you shook hands
with Anuj you might have noticed his wedding band ...'

'Is there something special about his wedding band?'

'You'd know if you have seen it.'

'Is it that conspicuous?'

'Yes, it is.' Bipin looked at Sharma who looked surprised.
Bipin subtly winked and gave a slight nod to let him carry
on and he'd explain later.

'Hmm ... it's a trick question, isn't it?' Arfy raised one
of his brows.

'How do you mean, sir?'

'For example, if I asked you whether your father still
beats his wife, that's a trick question, isn't it? You would
not say *yes* obviously, even if he beats your mother, but if
you say *no* it doesn't deny your old man once beat his wife.
You see what I mean?'

*Could this inspector ever respond to any question without
giving ridiculous analogies or telling long-winded irrelevant
anecdotes?*

'You don't know what kind of ring he wears, then?'
Bipin sounded desperate, but he didn't care what the
inspector thought. He'd know the truth in a minute.

Arfy made a face like he was on the periphery of a
profound thought. 'If I say the band is gold or platinum,

I might get it wrong. If I say, I didn't notice it I could get away under normal circumstances but that seems to be the trick question. How can a super-efficient senior police inspector like me not notice such things when he's just shaken hands with someone? You are a smart one, sonny boy, I have to give you that.'

'I'm hardly smart, sir, I just thought you might have noticed it because it's so different.'

'*Oligodactyly* – have you ever heard of the word?'

Another meaningless analogy was about to be forced down their throats. This inspector was a good-for-nothing.

'No, sir, what does it mean?'

'The word comes from Greek. You see *Oligo* means "few" and *Daktylos* means "fingers", so oligodactyly means fewer than five fingers or toes on a hand or foot. Your friend Ajay Shastri doesn't have a ring finger in his right hand, you smart-ass, sonny boy. Am I correct?'

Crestfallen, Bipin didn't know where to look. Meeting the inspector's eyes after he had tried to catch him was too painful. It was like playing bluff in cards and the only time you've asked someone for a show they'd told you the truth.

Shit! Shit! And more shit!

'Any more trick questions or was that all you had in your armoury, Mr Balan Desai?

Bipin didn't say a word. The inspector could have wrongly called him *baboon* instead of Balan and he still wouldn't dare to correct him. Not now!

'Quid pro quo,' Arfy started again. 'Now please don't tell me you haven't heard of this expression either.'

'I have,' Bipin could hardly find his voice.

'Good then. I answered your question, now you answer one of mine. Quid pro quo, right?'

'Senior Inspector Khan, my client and I need to confer on something important so could I ask you to step out and give us some time together please?'

'Why some time, take all the time you want, Mr Sharma, but let me put all the cards on the table before I leave. Without any prejudice, I promise to reduce the sentence of whichever of these two clowns tells me where the cash is. I hope I have made myself amply clear. The first one who speaks gets the deal.'

Sharma nodded.

Bipin nodded.

The inspector got up. 'And remember I need to close this today to take the papers to the court tomorrow to file a case and charge your client. Both of you put your heads together and do the maths before the other sonny boy and his lawyer pull the rug from under your feet. You've lost this hour quizzing me on pointless things when we could have had a serious discussion about Mr Birju Desai's future. Now, I'll be back in an hour. Just pray that your friend in the other room doesn't give me what I want in the next hour or your game is up. Got it?'

Sharma nodded.

Bipin nodded.

'My final piece of advice would be that you do not waste any more time than you already have. Goodbye for an hour or so, gentlemen.' Arfy got up and hit his toe against the table leg once more. He cringed, kicked the table, hurt himself yet again, turned around, cursed the poor table's sister and walked out without falling.

———

'I don't think your friend Anuj would have told the inspector that you borrowed his driving licence. It's good you didn't fall for Arfy's chicanery.'

'No way, I knew it was a lie, as I didn't borrow it.'

Before Bipin could explain how the inspector could have got hold of Anuj's driving licence, Sharma asked, 'what was that about Anuj's missing finger?'

Bipin told Sharma about the accident. If Arfy had said anything else it would have proved that he hadn't met Anuj, because *not* noticing a missing finger, especially when you shake hands with someone would have been a clear give away.

'It was a good try. I'm proud of the way you handled the question. Have you ever thought of becoming a lawyer?' Sharma smiled. In light of the tension in the room, the compliment was received with some relief. If he got out of this situation maybe there was a career for Bipin, he thought. To make money the honest way, the second time round?

'If it's a she—' Bipin said after a brief pause.

'If who's a she?'

'If Anuj's lawyer is a woman, it will be easier for you to find out who she is.'

'I realized that too, but that will only happen after I leave here, and Arfy said he wants to wrap this up today.'

'But that's not going to happen. He can't break me for sure, and I'm certain he won't be able convince Anuj to give up the cash and implicate me under any circumstances.'

'That's good to hear, but we must still be prepared for the worst. What if he has some other evidence?'

'You mean other than Anuj's driving licence?'

'Anuj's driving licence won't be enough to bring up a conviction in court. It's not even circumstantial evidence. People lose their wallets all the time. We can make a claim that Anuj lost his licence, and someone – whoever was involved in the heist – either intentionally or inadvertently dropped it at the crime scene, which puts the police on the wrong trail. But I have to say it was extremely careless of Anuj to …'

Bipin couldn't comprehend anything. Regardless of all the bullshit that the inspector had fed them, and how the truth could be twisted by a crafty lawyer like Sharma, it was clear how hapless they had been; of all the places that Anuj could have accidentally dropped his driving licence, he had mislaid it where it incriminated them the most. Destiny had chosen to be cruel to them yet again!

'Give me five minutes …' Bipin heard Sharma say and then he walked out for a cigarette.

16

FREE BIRDS

HISTORY IS AWASH WITH INSTANCES OF BANK ROBBERIES. In 1971, near Lloyd's Bank at Baker Street in London, a gang of thieves rented a shop two doors from the bank and dug a fifty-foot tunnel to provide them access to the vault in the basement where money and valuables worth three million pounds were stored.

One of the biggest bank robberies in India took place at the Miller Ganj Branch of Punjab National bank in Ludhiana, in 1987. Masterminded by none other than former police officer Labh Singh, fifteen men masqueraded as armed policemen and made off with six crore rupees.

In both the instances not a single person was injured.

Banks have been robbed before; banks could be robbed again.

The bottle of Old Monk long gone, Bipin and Anuj cooked stuffed omelettes. Anuj was in the mood to go out and purchase another bottle, but Bipin stopped him. 'We haven't looted the bank yet, we both have to go to work tomorrow.'

'Can we? Can we actually rob a bank and get away with it?'

The planning started then.

After hours of chatting frivolously, they both realized the other was equally enthused by the idea. Having seen too many heist movies, they knew what questions to consider.

But we have no experience.

We also don't have a police record, so if we leave no trace why would they come after us?

Someone will notice if we suddenly have money.

We will wait till the dust settles.

Where will we keep the money?

Safe house.

Where?

Some place far from here, where the rent is low.

'But why a bank?' asked Anuj.

'Because if you robbed any other place, you would have to sell your loot and convert it into cash anyway, so why not steal cash and keep it simple?'

'That is true, but won't a bank have more security?'

'It will. Also, one the biggest challenges in robbing a bank is that we would indirectly be stealing from the government, so yes the police will hunt more determinedly. You have a point. Let's go and get some more rum, this needs more planning.'

'I wish we had a phone, we could just call.'

'Soon we will have everything if our plan succeeds. We'll even get one of those new cellular phones some rich assholes flash around.'

The idea of robbing a bank was dropped by the time they finished the first drink from the new bottle. They realized they'd need some weapons if they needed to threaten even a solitary armed security guy outside a branch. And they didn't have the money to buy one, they didn't know where to buy one from and, most importantly, they didn't have the stomach to carry one.

'So we drop the idea, kill our dreams?' Anuj asked; he looked deflated.

'No way.'

'What then?'

'I have a better idea. Why don't we pour another drink and start all over again?'

'You know that I love you, my brother.'

As some wise old man had fittingly deduced: sentimentality turned to saccharine, and the effect was directly proportional to the amount of alcohol consumed. Bipin foolishly smiled. 'My brother from another mother, cheers!'

'Have you thought about getting married?' Anuj suddenly asked. Or was it the alcohol getting inquisitive?

'Who? Me?'

'Who else do you think I'm talking about? Manasi and I are already married to each other, aren't we? That leaves you ...'

'Who's going to marry me?'

'A girl.'

'Very funny.'

'I'm sure there must be a million girls in the suitable age group who would be happy to marry you.'

'Yeah, but I'm just an ordinary bloke who earns just about enough to make ends meet. Why would any girl be interested in marrying a loser like me?'

'I was financially a lot worse than you; I still am, and I still got married.'

'Your case was very different, Anuj.'

'Pray how? How was my case any different?'

'For starters, you are a good-looking lad, and you guys were in love with each other.'

'Have you never been in love?'

Bipin didn't respond. He took a swig from his drink hoping the moment would pass and the question would be forgotten.

'I asked you a question, pal. Have you never been in love?' Anuj repeated. He wasn't letting Bipin ignore his question.

'How many years have you known me for, Anuj? If I were in love with someone wouldn't you know it?

'What if I do know it?'

'Know what?'

'That you *were* in love ...'

'That's nonsense.'

'Come on, don't lie Bip-pin.' Anuj slurred, Old Monk taking over the conversation once again.

'Who was I in love with then, you tell me.'

'Manasi.'

'Rubbish.' An electric current ran through Bipin. *How much did his friend know about his romantic inclinations towards Manasi? Or that he peeped at them fornicating on his terrace. Bugger!*

'Don't lie. Manasi and I both know you loved herrr. I mean it's okay. She is a lovely girl and, unfortunately for you, I proposed firrrst so you didn't get a chance.'

'It's nothing like that.' Bipin could feel a rash of embarrassment rising up his neck. Thank god, Anuj was inebriated and wouldn't notice.

'Really? If we could clone Manasi wouldn't you rush to pr-propose your love to her?'

Bipin remained silent. He prayed Anuj would stop talking about this subject, even in the past tense. It was embarrassing to say the least.

'Hand on heart, my brrr-oth-err, tell me the trruth. Confide in me. I'm yourr frriend after all. We're all frriends, the three of us.' Besides the tongue slipping, Anuj was beginning to get animated. His hands moving, his eyebrows dancing up and down. It was an awkward moment. 'If you once had feelings for herr, why should you feel guilty? Unless you still have feelings for herr. Do you?'

'No, not at all. Okay, yes, I liked her ... I mean like her,' Bipin admitted seeing that his friend wasn't going to conclude the discussion if he didn't come clean. 'But I only see her as my friend and my friend's wife now. Don't you ever think I have any immoral feelings about Manasi, okay?'

'So if—' Anuj wanted to discuss something more, but Bipin was in no mood.

'End of discussion. I don't think we should talk on this sensitive issue ever again. Promise me.'

'I prrromise Bipin, but never stop loving us. You'rrre the only family we have.'

'I love you too, my brother.'

'We should buy a CD player when we get some extra cash, don't you think? Old Monk would taste so much better with Kishore Kumar.'

'You bet,' Bipin agreed but his friend had toppled off. *Thank god!*

Bipin stayed awake for a long time. The whole discussion about him being in love with Manasi had put him in an uncomfortable position. And the fact that Manasi knew about it and had even discussed it with Anuj was even more embarrassing.

17

JAILBIRDS

TIME IS A MAN-MADE CONSTRUCT.

Empty moments seemed to pass idly enough to shame a tortoise walking with a Zimmer frame, but during tense situations, time dissolved faster than a bubble in moving waters. The operative words were, of course, *seem to*, since the movement of time is an established constant. Sixty seconds in a minute tick, tock; sixty minutes in an hour tick, tock. However, to Bipin, this felt like an elaborate lie since SI Arfy Khan was back in the room before the inspector's crafty smile had disappeared from his retina. An entire hour had gone by. It was already past noon.

'What has this sonny boy decided in the past one hour?' Arfy asked even before his bottom touched the chair.

'Senior Inspector Khan, I have a question,' Sharma intervened.

'Et tu, Mr Sharma, are you asking a trick question now?'

'If you allow me, sir.'

'Let me guess: you want to know how I'm so good-looking and intelligent at the same time? I'm so glad you appreciate I'm not just a pretty face. It is rare to find beauty with brains together, but here I am. Some women friends even refer to me as debonair, could you believe that?'

There he goes again. God, this guy was a complete nutter.

'There is definitely some truth to that,' Sharma remarked, attempting appeasement.

'But ...?'

'But I still have a question.'

'You mean another question?'

'Yes, sir.'

'Go on, Mr Sharma. Ask and you shall not be disappointed.'

Something had changed. The devil appeared to be in a playful mood. What had taken place in the other room? What had Anuj told him? Like a flash the questions raced through Bipin's mind. The happiness plastered over the policeman's face gave him a feeling of discomfort. His heart beat a little faster. A lot faster, as a matter of fact, but he kept a poker face. He had heard that predators could sense fear in their prey. He tried to act as normally as he could lest Arfy should pounce on him.

'Besides the driving licence of Mr Anuj Shastri – that was allegedly recovered at the scene of some crime—'

'Ha ha!' Arfy burst out laughing. He raised his right palm and brought it down on the table with a thud. 'You make me laugh, Mr Sharma. Driving licence of Mr Shastri *allegedly recovered* at the scene of *some crime* ... really? I know you're an advocate, but may I request you talk a little less obliquely here, please?'

'I'm not sure I follow you, Senior Inspector Khan.'

'This sonny boy and the other sonny boy in the other room,' Arfy pointed towards the door and beyond, 'robbed a van full of cash, and the driving licence I showed you an hour ago was found inside that van.'

'Well, it's all conjecture, isn't it? There could be a hundred and one ways how a piece of plastic could be found at a location where its owner has never been. It wouldn't be the first time that one man's lost possession would have been carried by another individual, and—'

Arfy held his hand up to gesture Sharma to stop. 'Let's keep these arguments for the courtroom, Mr Sharma. I'm a policeman and hence, not so enlightened as an advocate like you, but I know you are well versed in turning a tangible piece of evidence into conjecture with your masterful spiel. We know for certain that it was the sonny boy here and Aman Shastri who were involved in the robbery, and all we need to know is: where is the cash now?'

'That's exactly my question, SI Khan. Without any evidence how can you ascertain that my client Bipin and Anuj were involved in the heist?'

'Mr Sharma, like I told you,' Arfy pointed at Bipin, 'his friend and his friend's lawyer aren't being as unhelpful as you are, so perhaps I'm better off talking to them than wasting time here. See you later.' Arfy stood up immediately, picked up his file, and got ready to leave. 'Is there anything else you want to ask or tell? This might be your last chance. I might not even bother to come back here. I'll ask Constable Bhim Singh to take this sonny boy back to the lock-up then …'

'Wait a minute.' Bipin's throat had run dry.

'Yes, my dear sonny boy. Do you want to know the colour of your friend's underwear now?'

'No, sir.'

'What is it then?' Arfy glanced at Sharma's watch to indicate he wasn't in any mood to squander any more time.

'What has Anuj told you?'

The familiar shrewd smile re-appeared on Arfy's face. 'Oh, a lot, where do I start?'

'Give me a hint, sir.'

'You want a hint? How about that your friend Alok Shastri knows you still have the hots for his wife, Malika Upadhaya?'

'You mean Manasi Upadhaya …'

'Yes.'

'That's not true.'

'What's not true?'

'I'm not in love with Manasi.'

'Isn't that why you went out of your way to bring them to your place to live when their parents threw them out? You had an ulterior motive, didn't you?'

'Bipin—' Sharma interposed.

'I didn't go anywhere. They came to me.'

'Bipin—' Sharma called his name again, a little louder this time.

'They didn't have a roof over their heads—'

'BIPIN, stop it, NOW,' Sharma shouted and put his arm over Bipin's to shake him out of the irrational anger that had taken him over. 'Just stop talking NOW,' Sharma repeated. Then he turned to Arfy, 'SI Khan, could you give us fifteen minutes please?'

'Like I said, I could give you the rest of the day off. Mr Balak Desai goes back to the lock-up for the night, and you can go to the cinema and watch *Rakshak*; you can even dance with Karisma Kapoor on that track … *Sundara Sundara* … great song, by the way. I love Karisma Kapoor, don't you?'

The look on Arfy's face suggested he might get up any moment and show some of Karisma Kapoor's dance moves; mercifully, the self-declared debonair senior inspector didn't go to that length.

What a total nutcase this police officer was. Un-fucking-believable!

Bipin looked at Sharma who nodded, then turned towards Arfy. 'Just give us fifteen minutes, sir, please.'

'Okay, maybe I'll take a break. I'll be back in fifteen minutes.' Arfy walked out without hitting or suggesting some other inbreeding relationships to the poor table. As he went out, they heard a loud thud. Perhaps he had indeed fallen right outside.

Advocate Sharma, judging that time was scarce, sacrificed his smoke break. Once the door closed, he gestured Bipin to remain quiet for a while. In the silence that ensued, they heard the footsteps recede. Safe. The red light blinked off again.

'You think they listen to us when we're here.'

'No, even the cameras should be switched off when it's just the lawyer and the client, but it would be foolish to trust this inspector.'

'Why?'

'He's lying, can't you see?'

Bipin nodded.

'You told me your friend would never cross you, then how could you believe Arfy Khan about anything?'

'If Anuj didn't tell him that how does he know that I once loved Manasi?'

'Did you?'

'Yes, but it was a long time ago. I don't love her now, I mean not in the way I loved her. She's been a friend since college, so it's that kind of love, you know. When friends become close, their gender becomes irrelevant, do you understand what I'm trying to say?' Bipin stopped. His own words sounded like someone guilty was trying to explain oneself. *Why?*

'Yes, I understand.'

'I forgot to ask you, did you manage to catch a glimpse of Anuj or his lawyer when you slipped out for a cigarette?'

'I know they are on the other side of the block. I tried to walk in there like I had lost my way, but a constable told me off.'

'Bhim Singh?'

'No, another one. I don't know his name.'

'I need to go to the toilet.'

'There's no point. They won't allow you anywhere near that room.' Sharma told Bipin how strict Arfy's warning to the constable had been with respect to keeping Bipin and Anuj away from each other since the know-it-all inspector anticipated toilets to be an excellent place for a criminal to hide notes meant for their accomplice. 'He has already thought about it.'

'I know that, but I really need to go to the toilet.'

'Okay then.' Sharma knocked on the door to call the constable. 'I'll take a short break too.'

———

Once back, Sharma reminded Bipin to not believe anything Arfy told him, irrespective of how plausible it sounded. The policeman, as they could see from his previous interaction, would not stop at anything to breach the fissures in Anuj and Bipin's friendship.

'If what I heard is correct, he's under tremendous pressure from the top to find the money.'

'I know. I just lost it completely because he was playing dirty.'

'He has barely begun, Bipin. If you trust your friend as much as you've told me, get a hold of yourself and this will all be over by tonight. Tomorrow morning will be forty-eight hours since your arrest, and he will have to go to court if he wants to keep you here. And once we are in court, leave it to the lawyers. There is no way Arfy, or even the commissioner of police, can stop you from meeting Anuj tomorrow.'

'Thank you, Mr Sharma.'

18

FREE BIRDS

THE TRIVIAL REMARK – *ROB A BANK* – UTTERED UNDER the influence of alcohol while passionately discussing the looming failures of life, might have come across as frivolous initially, but it was fast turning into a hard-boiled plot. In three simple iterations, *rob* a bank became *could we* rob a bank, which turned into *how could we* rob a bank, eventually giving way to *how could we get away* with robbing a bank?

With Manasi away until the delivery, Bipin and Anuj exchanged fresh and innovative ideas they'd thought up during the day after returning from work. Besides, the biggest worry with robbing a bank was the security. Banks always had an armed guard outside. Then, neither of the two knew where exactly the cash was kept in a bank – different banks could have different places where they locked up cash. And how much cash would there be? How long would they need inside the bank to collect it all?

What if someone pressed the panic button like they had seen in numerous films?

'I don't think we can rob a bank,' Anuj had all but given up. 'It was good to keep our minds occupied these past three days, but nothing more ... it's a shame because I had actually started planning how we'd live our lives afterwards. A big house, a few luxury cars, exotic foreign holidays, sending my child to a good school, but it wasn't meant to be—'

'Don't give up so soon. I have another idea; in fact, a better idea.'

'I am all ears.'

'Do you remember the retail company I worked for before this job?'

'The one with stores in Noida?

'Yes, RealStores.'

'What about it?'

'You know how many stores they have in Noida?'

'No, but I'm sure you will tell me.'

'Thirty-five,' I checked today.

'So we go with a gun and rob some of them instead of a bank?'

'Okay, let's have a drink first, only one each since we have work tomorrow, but it will help you relax and understand my plan better.'

'You're the boss.' Anuj got up, poured two fingers of Old Monk in glasses, topped them up with cola and ice and returned to the terrace where they sat.

'Cheers!'

'Cheers!

'Since I was an apprentice I've worked in half of those stores, while being rotated around to learn different roles. I worked on ordering, stocking, merchandising, tills and accounts. Do you have any idea what the average turnover of these stores is?'

'Not a clue, buddy.'

'The big stores turn over a lakh and twenty-five a day, and small ones average around seventy-to-eighty thousand per day.'

Anuj whistled.

'It sounds like a lot, but it truly isn't because televisions, computers and other electronics are big-ticket items. And that's not all; the cash isn't transported to the bank on a daily basis; it's stored in a safe that can be accessed only if three senior members of the team come together to punch in their respective codes and use three separate keys. No single person can access it individually—'

'So how do we access the safe?'

'Wait a minute my friend, do you have a calculator?'

'No, what do I need one for?'

'Wait.' Bipin went in to fetch his Casio digital diary. 'Okay my friend, here we go. Come close.' With Anuj close enough to see the screen, Bipin continued. 'For the sake of our calculations, let's assume that big and small stores are a fifty-fifty split, so the average turnover of big and small stores would be ...' He keyed in the numbers:

1,25,000 + 75,000 / 2 = 1,00,000
'Then multiply it by 35 stores.'
1,00,00 X 35 = 35,00,000

'Oh my god,' Anuj's eyes widened when he saw the amount.

'That's not all, my friend. The company policy is not to keep the cash in the local safes for more than three or four days.'

'What does that mean?'

'The cash is transported by a van that makes two trips a week to take the cash to the head office on Barakhamba Road where the accounts are verified and balanced by the bookkeepers before the money is deposited in a bank. It's an outdated process, but the store's largest shareholders are the Singhals, an old family, who are more comfortable with these antiquated methods than depositing the money directly.'

'Don't they understand the risks?'

'I'm sure they do, but they've been doing it for decades without any issues. Plus, I think they do this to evade taxes – this way, they can choose to report only half the sales, you see?'

'Really?'

'Anyway, as I was saying … on Monday the van takes the cash earned between Friday and Sunday, and it carries the money received between Monday and Thursday on Friday mornings.'

'So what does that mean for us?'

'We target the van on Monday morning. The sales over the weekends with the three days' cash should be—'

$$35,00,000 \text{ x } 3 = 1,05,00,000$$

'... the amount,' Bipin continued once they had both seen and absorbed the figure of one crore and five lakhs on the Casio screen, '... may vary, as it's retail – but I don't think it'll be vastly different from our calculation. If anything, we'll get more than that, since I know sales figures are always a lot higher over the weekends.'

'One fucking crore?'

'Could be ... could be even more.'

'Wow, this sounds better than a bank robbery.'

'Also, I am confident that the currency notes coming in are not numbered or marked in any way, though I'm not certain. Maybe they are, but there is another negative too.'

'What's that?'

'The currency will be in all kinds of denominations, including coins.'

'Why do we care, it is still money isn't it?'

'That much currency would be large in volume,' Bipin pointed out. He drained his glass and poured another drink for both of them.

'How big a suitcase do we need?'

'Let's calculate. A single five hundred rupee note ... *hic* ... weighs approximately one-point-one-five grams, so if the entire money was in five-hundred rupee notes, we'll have approximately twenty-thousand notes – for ease of calculation let's imagine the sum is one crore. And that would weigh ...' Back to Casio:

20,000 x 1.15 = 23,000

'... twenty-three kilograms.' Bipin looked up.

Another generous serving of Old Monk was poured and devoured in two sips.

'That *ish* not much.' Anuj slurred happily.

'But, the cash will not be in the largest denomination. It will have ... *hic* ... hundreds, fifties, twenties, tens, and smaller and, ergo, the total volume might be fifty-thousand notes and weigh more like fifty kilos – we can't ... *hic*... know until we see it; it could vary from one consignment to the other.'

'That sh ... shouldn't take more than three suitcases, we can check by cutting newspaper into size of currency note-sh—'

'We can, but we shall do that ... *hic* ... later.'

'Why not now?'

'You know why I love you, Anuj?' Engrossed in the discussion and calculations, they had completely lost track of how many drinks they'd had. The syrupy emotions got to the forefront again. 'You are such a simpleton.'

'Why, brother?'

'Because you are so trusting, my friend; while the cash can be packed in three large suitcases, not once did you ask me ... *hic* ... how will we get the cash out of the van?'

'Good point, brother. Tell ... tell me.'

But Bipin's eyes had started closing, his head was rolling; he was high on Old Monk and the thought of one crore rupees. 'Tomorrow ... *hic*!'

19

FREE BIRDS

'I'M CALLING IN SICK TODAY,' BIPIN TOLD ANUJ WHEN THEY woke up the next morning.

'I'll do the same. Munna ji is very understanding.'

They went out and made calls to their respective workplaces and returned carrying some more alcohol. The piquant taste of Old Monk was still lingering on their tongues; the lust for luxuries just added to it.

'So how do we do this?' Anuj asked. 'I'm sure you've thought of something.'

Bipin gestured to Anuj to come to the dinette – the only counter they had in the barsaati. He pulled out a map of Delhi and Noida and spread it in front of them, and the two got down to some serious planning.

Sometimes conscience takes a back seat. At other times, people ignore the little voice inside them to pay heed to their desires instead. In their drunken stupor – that the two friends had brought upon themselves in Manasi's absence – the thought of pointless drudgery and the lure of easy money was enough to convince them that a little aberration from the rules of society was justified. And it all sounded plausible: one big score and they'd be over the line forever; it'd be a piece of cake. The amount was huge, and they weren't going to splurge and lose it all. They were normal middle-class people who appreciated the value of each rupee. They'd safeguard it, invest it wisely, and live off it for the balance of their lives. Hitherto suppressed dreams would finally see the light of the day. The endless stream of struggle would dissipate.

'When I worked there about a year ago, the cash van's last stop in Noida, before going on to Connaught Place, used to be in Sector 18.'

'We need to intercept the cargo somewhere between Sector 18 and Delhi—'

'Wait a minute,' Bipin suddenly recalling something. 'RealStores also had a small outlet in Mayur Vihar Phase I; en route to Connaught Place, it used to stop there as well, but I wouldn't know for sure, since it wasn't the remit of our team—'

'Why?

'Because it was in Delhi. For some internal political reason that store, albeit small, was managed directly by the employees at head office. We'll have to find out.'

'How do we do that?'

'We will have to do a recce to confirm it. Follow the van a few times when it's on the rounds. If that is still the case, we have to stop the van when it leaves Mayur Vihar and before it crosses the river.'

'So it has to be on the Nizamuddin Bridge then,' Anuj said. He got up to make a drink.

'It's only noon,' Bipin pointed at the clock. 'We should work on the plan first. If we keep drinking, we won't be able to finalize the plan.'

'Haven't we already?'

'Of course not, please leave the drink, and come back. We need to plan it in detail.'

'What now?'

'The recce, the vehicle or vehicles, how will we intercept the van? The driver isn't going to just stop if we ask him to stop. Where do we go from there? There are a lot of gaps to fill …'

A few hours passed by like minutes. Both friends agreed that prevention was better than cure. The old maxim, *awareness of danger is the best insurance*, rang true. So, should anything go out of kilter at any point, they decided to abandon the field and walk away. Nothing gained, but they'd lose nothing either. What could possibly go wrong?

Anuj and Bipin decided to take a few days off – Mondays and Fridays to follow the van. Working for Munna ji, Anuj had learnt a valuable skill: he could open and jump-start any car within minutes. They had to use a different car each time to ensure that the van driver would not figure out he was being trailed.

But they couldn't take the same days off on successive weeks. At any rate, they couldn't put their plan into motion at a week's notice. They needed more planning. More tools.

'What tools?' Anuj asked when Bipin mentioned them.

'Disguises or masks. I'm thinking disguises, masks are too conspicuous.'

'Okay, that makes sense.'

'We need some kind of weapon, at least a fake one.'

'What for?'

'We might need it – in case we need to threaten the driver.'

'Does he, the driver, carry a weapon?'

'Not that I know of,' Bipin recalled from memory. 'The whole operation relies on discreetness. No one knows about the van carrying the cash except those who work in accounts. The van looks ordinary – no logo, no marks; no one can suspect it carries over a crore in cash—'

'What is the make of the van?'

'I don't know. Does that matter?'

'Yes, we'll need to find something equally large to shift the bags from the van to our vehicle, won't we?'

'Silly me, I never thought about that. See, we need to plan this thing very minutely, every step of the way. But … if we intercept the van, we should make our getaway in that van; that will eliminate the need to transfer the money into suitcases in the open.'

'Brilliant idea, my friend. We need to make another drink to commend you for this,' Anuj insisted.

'Just one, and then we get back to planning.'

'You're the boss.' Anuj got up to make drinks.

'What about Manasi?' Bipin asked.

'What about her?'

'Will you tell her?'

'No way.'

'Then what's the plan?

'Manasi will be at her parents' place until January. She'll be more comfortable there … I mean … I don't mean that it's uncomfortable here, but we can't give her the support that her mother can provide, you see? We have to do this while she is not here.'

'I guess so, and I can understand. Actually, if you don't want to tell her about this, it's best she stays there and it will also give us time to plan freely.'

'But we need to be careful not to leave any plan or maps lying around. She has a spare key so she can come and go anytime. And the last thing we want is for her to come across something we've left around carelessly if she visits while we are at work.'

'Cheers!'

'Cheers!'

The second drink followed the first without interruption. The discussion carried on.

'And we need to find some place to hide the cash,' Bipin recommended.

'Why?'

'You don't want to be seen with more money than you

can explain. If we suddenly started driving imported cars, the neighbours would smell a rat. It's dangerous to attract attention to ourselves.'

'So what do we do?'

'We'll have to find a place and hide the money until the investigation is over. If the heat doesn't go down, we might have to move the cash abroad through *hawala*.'

'Do you know someone who could do that for us?'

'No, but I'm sure once we have the money, it won't be difficult to find one. I'll talk to a few people and find out, don't worry. Money laundering is done all over the world; we'll work something out. We cannot hide the cash here, so I was thinking of renting a place.'

'Rent another place? Where will we get the money from?'

'I don't know that either, but we will have to set aside some money to *invest* in this venture, if we want to do it properly.'

'Hmm …'

'Are you absolutely sure you want to do this? However few, there are some some risks,' Bipin asked.

'One hundred percent yes. Are you having second thoughts, by any chance?'

'Of course not, I'm fully on board.'

Greed always finds a reason to take over the astute mind. At the very least, it furnishes practical options to rationalize things. They wound up the discussion after a while when the conversation started to get maudlin again. Anuj had convinced himself he was doing this for his unborn child and his wife. Bipin was happy; he believed this plan was in everyone's interest. They were one, weren't they? Three friends, albeit separate families, they were one organism. One for all and all for one; they would sink or sail together.

———

Manasi's tentative delivery date was in the third week of January, which gave Bipin and Anuj four months to execute their plan. Once the baby arrived, the circumstances would change. To begin with, there wouldn't be enough space for the four of them in the barsaati; Anuj and Manasi would have to move out, if not immediately, then soon after. Although that would leave this pad as an exclusive place to make plans, since Manasi would no longer have access, but with a newborn at home, how much time would Anuj have? There'd be constraints on his free time. The two agreed it was best to carry out their plans before the baby arrived. It was now or never, but 'never' was not an option. If they failed to follow through this plan, they would regret it forever. What about their unrealized dreams? Anuj's daughter or son would be stuck in a middle-class life just like them.

The first reconnaissance trip from Noida to Connaught Place established that RealStores hadn't changed the mode of cash collection and transportation from stores since Bipin had left.

Tick!

The van, albeit nondescript, wasn't one of the off-the-shelf varieties; it was custom-built on a Tata 407 Chassis. A cab in front had a light dent on the bumper with heavy, secured twin doors in the rear. It was strong and fireproof – the rear panels were reinforced steel that were painted white to look ordinary. The sides were bare except a few scrapes and scratches; it looked like it could certainly do with a lick of paint, but the owners clearly didn't want the van to be conspicuous. They could not risk some punter nicking an immaculate-looking van and unwittingly winning the jackpot inside. The two friends tailed it one afternoon until it was parked without supervision, which gave Anuj time to investigate the exterior panels. It was built with twice the gauge used by other commercial vans of a similar ilk. 'A vault on wheels,' Anuj commented. The big guns at the store weren't lackadaisical when it came to securing their cash. But since Bipin and Anuj's plan didn't entail cutting through the sheet metal, it wouldn't be an issue.

Tick!

The driver was the sole person inside at all times. A dark, balding man, fortyish and well-built, he had clearly been employed for his loyalty and not his looks. He had been doing this job for at least a decade and nothing had ever gone missing. He didn't even wear a uniform – just an average-looking man who would not attract attention. The duller the driver and van, the safer the cargo. He got down at every outlet, walked in, carried the parcel out alone, dumped it in the back of the van, locked the doors and drove off casually as if he had just bought fish from the market. He did not carry any weapons. At least, nothing was apparent. It would seem suspicious if the driver of a private van was armed with anything more than a baton or, at best, a knife.

Tick!

And the van followed the same route twice a week. There were no diversions. The only variations were on account of traffic. As anticipated, the last stop was a small store in Mayur Vihar Phase I.

Tick!

If they had to intercept the van, they would have to do it after the van turned left on Nizamuddin Bridge and before it turned right after the bridge. A distance of approximately five kilometres, it would take a van travelling at 50 kmph approximately six minutes to complete. Add another nine-or-ten minutes for traffic, and they had fifteen minutes to carry out their operation.

Tick!

Anuj had already proved a few times that he could break-in and hotwire a vehicle in minutes. They could pick up and change vehicles as and when the situation required.

Tick!

The big question remained unanswered: how would they stop the van? Forcefully pushing it onto the side of the road with another van would alert the other drivers on the road. Thumbing for a ride wouldn't work as the van driver would be under instructions from the owners not to stop and offer lifts to strangers. The driver would certainly not break the rule for one or two young men. A scantily clad female might have worked but they didn't know any women who would help them. Also, they had decided not to involve anyone else and ergo that too was a no-go. Would a driver stop to help if he saw a broken-down vehicle? Extremely unlikely. No one in their right minds would stop their vehicle to help change a tyre if they were carrying a large amount of cash.

'But, what if his own van breaks down? Wouldn't he be forced to stop and ask for help?' Anuj asked.

'How do you mean?'

'We've witnessed that he leaves the van unattended when he goes into the stores – what if we sabotage the vehicle somehow to break down?'

'But how do we arrange a time-related failure? We want him to start his journey from Mayur Vihar and break down while he is on the Nizamuddin Bridge? Not before or after.'

'When he goes into the last store in Mayur Vihar to collect cash, I'll slip under the vehicle and cut the brake line—'

'Wouldn't he know as soon as he starts to drive?'

'No, I won't punch a huge hole, just big enough for

the brake fluid to start draining gradually; slow enough for him to realize something's wrong after only a few kilometres, and by then he'll be on the bridge.'

'What if—'

'Don't worry. A small leak would give itself away some time before total failure, so he won't crash; he'll be able to slowly bring the vehicle to a halt.' Anuj said to assuage his friend's unspoken concern.

'Do you know how big the brake fluid tank in this van is, and how precise a hole you need for the driver to take notice when he's on the bridge?'

'No, but I'll find out.'

'Don't ask Munna ji,' Bipin warned.

'Of course, not. I'll figure it out myself. Similar vehicles come into our garage for repairs all the time. The next time, I'll check the size of their brake fluid tank. And I can always circumvent and ask questions to find out the rest.

Tick!

Since Manasi was away, their expenses had gone down too. The two friends decided to live frugally to save more since the last part of their plan required money. The stolen loot had to be hidden somewhere. The barsaati had already been ruled out. They needed another place.

'Should we look for another barsaati around here?'
Anuj asked.

'No. We should keep it as far as possible from us.
Should something go wrong, nobody can trace it back to
us. I'm thinking of Gurgaon.'

'Why Gurgaon?'

'Because the rent for a room in Delhi will be the same
we'd pay for an entire house in Gurgaon. And a house will
allow independent access without other people seeing us
in the building.'

'But why Gurgaon?'

'Because we will flee with the loot from Noida; it's safer
to take the cash across the state borders.'

'That makes sense.'

'We need to work out our disguises first so when either
one of us rents the house the estate agent or the landlord
won't know our real face either.'

'When do we need to do this?'

'Ideally, we should do it as soon as possible. If we rent
it now, and the robbery in Delhi or Noida takes place after
a few months, there's no way for someone to connect the
two – not that anyone should think we've rented the house
to hide money from a heist. But I'd rather pay rent for an
additional two months than raise any suspicion.'

'But we won't live there, will we?'

'No, you or I will need to get a fake ID to hire the
premises under a false name and tell the landlord or

whoever that we are waiting for the family to move from someplace else but we want the home to be ready before the family arrives in town. We can make some excuse later why the move is delayed, should somebody ask, although why would anyone bother?'

'It's October, so do we rent from this month-end or from early November?'

'Let's start looking at classifieds for available properties in Gurgaon.'

Tick!

'What about the weapon?'

'Fake weapon,' Bipin corrected. Diwali is on thirtieth of this month. We'll pick up a top-of-the-line model.'

'The *patake-wali* pistol?'

'Some of them look unbelievably real; you won't be able to tell the difference, believe me.'

'But they must weigh a lot less?'

'You aren't planning to hand over the gun to the driver to let him check the weight, are you?'

Tick!

'You've thought of everything,' Anuj said, visibly impressed.

'I've been thinking about it every night and making mental notes.'

'What else have you thought of?'

'We need disguises.'

'That should be an easy one to accomplish. What do you want to be? Batman, Spiderman or Superman?'

'Someone who does not wear their underpants over their trousers.'

The two burst into laughter.

Tick!

The second round of preparations started to fill in any gaps in the plan that they might have previously overlooked.

Finally it started to sound like an impregnable plan.

20

JAILBIRDS

SI ARFY KHAN RETURNED TO THE ROOM IN FIFTEEN minutes like he had promised. He wore stylish glasses with a bluish wayfarer frame this time. 'Sorry, I was reading some legalities to confirm things.' He sat down, made himself comfortable by crossing his right leg over his left and took the glasses off. Then almost on impulse, he started tapping the earpiece against his teeth: *tic, tic!* Just another annoyance in the room that was already filled with tension.

He gave them a moment, then looked at Mr Sharma and asked: 'Has the sonny boy here decided to talk anything that makes sense now?'

'We don't know what you mean by that exactly, SI Khan,' Bipin responded, his voice a mere whisper.

'Congratulations, by the way.' Arfy turned his attention from Sharma to Bipin, 'You are a reluctant uncle.'

'What do you mean?'

'Arup and Maanvi had a baby girl. Very cute.'

'Why do you call me a reluctant uncle?' By now Bipin was proficient enough to comprehend that Arfy meant *Anuj* and *Manasi*, and it was pointless to highlight or correct the daft inspector. He seemed incapable of processing or keeping track of the names of people he was dealing with; or perhaps he was distracted, his brain out to lunch somewhere.

'Because from all the information that I've gathered so far, sonny boy, you would've very much wanted to be the father of her child,' Arfy was evidently taking pleasure in tormenting Bipin. 'Ain't I right?'

'That's sheer nonsense.' Bipin could feel the hair bristle on his nape with rage, but he shut up after his initial response.

'Did you never make out with Manasi?'

'No.' Bipin was aghast at the question. 'This is so out of order ...' Bipin stared at Sharma like a schoolboy asking his teacher to stop a bully.

'If you say so ...'

'SI Khan, can you please speak more clearly? What does my client have to do to get out of this place?'

Arfy ignored Sharma's question. Instead he kept talking to Bipin: 'How long will both of you hold back?'

'We're not holding back anything at all. We are not who you're looking for, sir; this is some kind of misunderstanding.'

'Everyone I meet is either a comedian or a genius. You

don't seem like a genius because you made elementary mistakes and got caught within days of the robbery; so you have be some kind of a comedian. Does all this look like a joke to you?'

Look at yourself, you seem more like a comedian than me, you bloody clown, Bipin wanted to yell.

'How does this conversation help you, SI Khan?' Sharma urged.

'Mr Sharma, do you know the old story – wait a minute, I think it was also in some film – where a girl challenged two chess grandmasters to play chess with her simultaneously?'

There he goes again!

Both Sharma and Bipin looked agape. They had serious issues on their minds and this silly inspector insisted on telling random stories, which didn't even seem relevant to the case at hand.

Was there no way to gag this inspector?

'Oh, I can see in your faces that you've never heard it. So, a gorgeous woman asks two grandmasters to sit in separate rooms and plays chess against both. And wins against both. Do you know how?'

Arfy must have construed their blank looks as interest in his story and ergo he continued: 'It was quite simple actually. She let the first grandmaster play the first move, then repeated the first grandmaster's move with the other player. She then waited for the second grandmaster's move and did the same thing. If you're bright enough, you'll understand she was actually playing one master against the other on two separate chessboards.' Arfy clapped his hands and guffawed loudly. 'She was a genius. Isn't that a fantastic story?'

Neither of the two men spoke, but they understood why he had told them the story. That was exactly what he was doing – playing Bipin against Anuj and vice versa. In that moment Arfy seemed more like an evil villain than the comedian Bipin had initially thought him to be.

You're not even half as amusing as you think you are! But Bipin did not let the words appear on his lips.

Sweat broke out on his forehead. He had been calm all along, confident in his friend's loyalty. But it was apparent SI Arfy Khan was playing dirty now. If he was attempting to provoke Bipin by insinuating he was somehow romantically or sexually involved with Manasi, and admittedly succeeding, how would Anuj react?

Shit! Shit! Shit!

Bipin wondered how Anuj would respond to the inspector's slimy tricks. It was one thing to be accused of a romantic liaison with an old friend who was now another close friend's wife, but an altogether different matter if Arfy was, however obliquely, was insinuating to Anuj that he was a cuckold while his own friend, whom he trusted like a brother, was intimately involved with his wife, the mother of their newborn child. Bipin knew that it would not take much for Anuj to flare up if he even remotely believed Arfy's wild accusations. 'You can't do that,' Bipin heard himself say it aloud.

'I can't do *what*, sonny boy?' Arfy asked.

'I meant you shouldn't do this, this is unethical.'

'Oh, so now I need an ethics class from you? You make me laugh, sonny boy. Imagine my moral science teacher is a convicted thief—'

'SI Khan, my client has not been convicted yet, please note.'

'Let me rephrase, a soon-to-be-convicted thief, does that sound better, Advocate Sharma?'

'He's accused on flimsy charges. There may or may not be a conviction – it depends on whether the court believes your charges.'

'I apologize,' Arfy said with a sly smile. 'But your time is up.' He got up, pulled out a pocket watch and checked the time: 'it's two-thirty now. I'll close shop at five-thirty sharp, but I bet I won't have to wait that long. Your friend Amit Shastri is quite warmed up to squeal—'

'Wait a minute,' Bipin blurted out, shaking. He knew Anuj could break at the inspector's tactics.

'Wait for what, sonny boy?'

'What if I tell you where the cash is?'

'That's not enough; you have to tell me where the cash is before your friend tells me.'

'Okay, if I tell you right now—'

'Both of you have some kind of telepathic connection, I have to admit. You sing the same tune, at the same time. Just a while back, neither of you was willing to cooperate at all, and now both of you are eager to spill the beans, which is such a pity. Perhaps what my bosses say is true: I'm a poor investigator who wasn't able to work out how you operate. Maybe you guys are too clever for me or maybe I'm too thick.' He shook his head like he was surprised. 'Anyway, like I told you, your time is up for now, and it's your friend's turn to divulge. Let me go and talk to him first. Maybe you've missed the proverbial bus.' He winked.

'Okay, we understand,' Sharma chimed in. 'But what's on offer?'

'Whoever discloses the location – and there's no agreement if we don't find the cash there – gets a reduced sentence.'

'Reduced by how much?'

'Why don't we do the following: I go and talk to the other sonny boy. If he and his lawyer have worked out a better proposition for us, this discussion is meaningless, purely theoretical. If what they ask for is unreasonable and I reject their offer, then I return and you get another chance. I'm sorry but I have to be fair.' The same sly know-it-all smile appeared on the devil's face. 'Now, think, and think fast because I'll be back in under an hour to ask what you're looking for. But if you two decide on anything that might interest me quickly, Mr Sharma can ask Constable Bhim Singh to slip me a note in the other room, and I'll try to come here as soon as prudent.' Arfy turned and bumped into the door. He stood massaging his forehead for a minute; then he slammed the door shut, and walked away.

Sharma walked out for a smoke almost immediately without uttering a word.

The red camera light went off after a few seconds. Arfy had ratcheted up the pressure, the worry, the tension, and Bipin lost his composure. He broke down like a schoolboy. He could empathize how Anuj must feel: his baby girl was born while he was in prison with the inspector accusing him of being a cuckold. Anuj would certainly retaliate. If he was put in Anuj's position he would too.

Well, this had got ugly ...

———

Bipin rubbed his face to wipe off his tears. His throat was constricted, his voice choked. Advocate Sharma was back in the room after his cigarette break. There was little point in putting up a brave front when his voice would give him away anyway.

'What were you thinking?' Sharma asked, without referring to Bipin's emotional outburst.

'I think Anuj is in a far greater quandary than me, isn't he? He's just become a father and he hasn't even seen his little girl. Top that emotional state with this inspector's harsh allegations. I won't blame him if he breaks down.'

'So do you no longer have confidence in your friend, then?'

'I'm not sure. Although Anuj is not crafty, he could

naturally have a knee-jerk reaction to Arfy's malicious comments about his wife and me. And the inspector might convince Anuj into believing I had buried intimate feelings towards Manasi, or a relationship, or harboured ill feelings towards either or both of them for that reason.'

'So?' Sharma continued to distract Bipin from bursting into tears again.

'So how can I trust him to do the right thing?'

'I get your point. So what do you want to do?'

'I don't know. What do you suggest I do?'

'In such circumstances, it is usually a good plan to shoot before your rival shoots you down.'

'You mean give away the information Arfy wants or before Anuj decides to tell him everything and gets his sentence reduced?'

'That's the only way forward if you've now lost trust in your friend,' Sharma said matter-of-factly. Emotions had no part to play with such high stakes.

'Could we bargain for a complete pardon for me in exchange for the location of the money.'

'Would you also become a state witness and testify against Anuj?'

'Do I have to?'

'I'm sure SI Arfy will demand it as part of the exchange.'

'Could I get a complete pardon then?'

'A complete pardon is unforeseeable, I have to admit. Arfy cannot lie that you weren't involved at all, especially since Anuj's lawyer knows the truth as well as I do. No judge in any court would allow you to walk away scot free.

But, we can request a reduced prison sentence for you.'

'How short or long would it be?'

'I cannot assure anything because it is not in my power, but once the cash has been recovered using your information, considering there are no manslaughter or grievous-bodily-harm charges, and no past police record for either of you – the court shouldn't sentence you for more than five to seven years in prison. Given the precedence, the sentence won't be very harsh.'

'Seven years? That's a long time.' Bipin's voice trembled with fear. The gravity of his predicament was beginning to penetrate his brain, and an ominous feeling washed over him. He was reminded of the horror stories about prisons again. He wouldn't survive that long.

'I know it sounds long, but you guys planned a heist – it demonstrates criminal intentions – and got away with more money than most people make in their lifetimes. You also injured a person in the process, and the penalty is always in line with the gravity of the crime.'

'So what do you think is reasonable to ask Arfy?'

'Well, if you provide the right information and we offer you as a state witness, I'm quite confident your sentence could be halved or even less than that. If Anuj's lawyer is smart enough, I'm guessing she won't let the prosecutor ask for more than five years of custody, so you could be out in anything between twenty-four to thirty months.'

'That's still long.'

'It is. But, trust me, I'll haggle hard to get a better deal.'

'Thank you, Mr Sharma.'

'Well, *thank you* is all I'll get now, isn't it? If you tell the police where the money is hidden, I won't get any part of the sum you promised me. And I've already sunk borrowed money into this investigation. I am stuck in this situation too.' Sharma looked dejected, and justifiably so.

But Bipin's mind had started floating like a fickle-minded butterfly, jumping from one flower to another. Thoughts flitted through his mind faster than it was capable of processing or analysing them, as though he had driven into torrential rain with broken windshield wipers. He found it impossible to concentrate. He had enough troubles clouding him; the last thing he cared about was if Sharma got his share of the loot or not.

If Anuj broke before him, Bipin would understand; Bipin would make peace with himself. In a way wouldn't it be the right thing? Poor Anuj would get out of the tangle; he had a wife and a newborn baby whom he hadn't seen yet. Who did Bipin have to go back to? No one, he thought, awash with emotions once again. Then he suddenly realized the other part of the puzzle. He remembered warning Anuj not to leave the safe house while he was away, but Anuj had still gone against his advice. It was perfectly reasonable for Anuj to have felt anxious when Bipin hadn't returned in a couple of hours to buy food and drinks: how long had he said, fifteen, twenty minutes tops? Maybe Anuj stepped out of the house to make a call to Manasi and found out he'd had a baby daughter? That must have prompted him to rush to Munirka where Inspector Arfy or his team lay in wait to arrest him instead. How must poor Anuj feel? Trapped. Maybe they didn't let him meet or even see his daughter.

Bastards!

Just when it seemed they were over the edge, they had slipped hard. Sank on the shores, as they said. What could be worse? His reverie was broken when he heard his name.

'Bipin, do you agree with my proposal?'

'Yes … yes, sir.' He didn't much care one way or the other; any outcome would be better than the uncertainty. In the last few minutes, he had convinced himself that, although he wanted to get out of the jail as soon as he could, if Anuj revealed the location of the cash in exchange for an advantageous deal, he wouldn't hold it against his friend. But he wouldn't give up his right to fight either.

'Okay, then I'll send SI Khan a note that we want to see him before he takes any decision,' Sharma announced and scurried out.

21

FREE BIRDS

Sunday, 12 January 1997

THE DAY BEFORE THE HEIST, ANUJ WENT TO SPEND TIME with Manasi at her mother's place. For their plan to succeed, it was paramount that they filled in as many fissures as they could possibly anticipate. The unpredictable ones would need to be dealt with on the fly. But it was vital that they told Manasi a believable story because they didn't want her to visit the barsaati when they weren't there and get worried. Worse still, get alarmed and call the police, which would jeopardize their plan.

'We're going off for a few days, just Bipin and I,' Anuj told her casually.

'Where to?'

'Rajasthan. We will drive there, spend a couple of days and return. Just a short vacation for the boys.'

'And why do the boys need a vacation and not me?' Manasi had a point.

'Manasi, we've lived with Bipin for a long time, so I thought I will take him out for a short break to thank him for all that he's done for us. If you wish, we can postpone it until the baby is born, and go together. No big deal. I'm sure he'll understand ...'

'Have you already discussed it with him?'

'Of course, I had to ask him to take time off work, didn't I?'

'Then you guys should go ahead; I was only asking. I'm sure we can go again later, but you're right. He has done so much for us. I'm glad you thought about it; this is why I love you so much, Anuj.'

'No seriously, we can go later if you—'

'No baba, once the baby arrives,' Manasi rubbed her belly to accentuate it, 'there will be too much going on in our lives for the next six-to-nine months. I think you guys should go for a short break now. We can take a longer vacation after the summer.'

'I promise, or we'll go abroad like we discussed.'

'Exactly! How're you two travelling?'

'Munna ji has loaned me a car, so we'll drive.'

'Please drive safely, Anuj.'

'Yes, ma'am. We'll leave tomorrow morning, so we should be back by Friday or Saturday. Don't let the baby come out before I return, OK?'

'Come closer, give me a hug.'

Monday, 13 January 1997

05:00 a.m.

They woke up early. Truth be told, anxiety kept them up most of the night. After three, four months of planning, they could not afford to stumble on a single step so they consciously stayed away from alcohol the previous night. If all went to plan, the rest of their lives would be nothing short of a dream.

'Are you ready?' Bipin asked. He was an old man for the day – fiftyish – with lots of grey hair, long sideburns, and a thick grey moustache. He wore large retro-nerd, thick black square frames with dark glasses.

'I am.' Anuj was wearing dark aviators and a baseball cap with a long peak that shadowed his face all the way to his nose.

They carried a small toolkit Anuj had put together for the operation, which contained pins to pick locks, cables to hot-wire and some other basic tools.

To any passers-by, they looked like an old man with a young one; maybe father and son or an uncle with his nephew. No one would think the two were the same age. And that's what they had planned for. They left home early, around 5:30 a.m., to avoid being seen in their disguises by any of the neighbours. Both wore nondescript blue jeans, sneakers and old T-shirts, mottled with grease marks.

After walking for a kilometre Bipin waited as Anuj managed to jump-start a Fiat Uno. They threw their bags into the rear and drove off towards Noida. 'Shit,' Anuj was exasperated after they'd barely gone a few kilometres.

'What happened?'

'There's no petrol in this car.'

'We cannot go into a petrol station to refill. They might have a camera. Nevertheless, a Fiat Uno is the wrong car for our plan – there aren't too many of them around so someone might notice it. Let's drive into Lajpat Nagar and look for a Maruti instead.'

Twenty-five minutes later, they were on the Nizamuddin Bridge in a white Maruti 800 heading towards Noida.

07:00 a.m.

Their schedule for the day was simple. They'd pick up something to eat, change the car once, maybe twice. It was a good idea to switch vehicles, because by the time the owner lodged a complaint to the police, a notice was issued to the traffic police and the hunt for the car had started, a couple of hours would have passed already. By then, they would have dumped that vehicle and picked up another one, repeating the same cycle. The first couple of hours were relatively safe in a stolen car unless a suspicious policeman stopped you for some inane reason and who might smell a rat. Ergo, never jump a red light in a stolen car.

Around seven o'clock, the two friends stopped at a roadside where a cart-vendor was cooking masala omelettes. There were a lot of people picking up on-the-go omelettes inside buns wrapped in newspaper. A crowd around the cart implied that the vendor wouldn't be paying attention to the patrons; he appeared busy with his head down, breaking, whisking, frying the eggs, heating the buns, packing the omelettes, collecting the cash, rendering change. Bipin collected their order and carried them to the car. Fortunately, the windows of the car had a dark film and the two of them rolled them up and munched on their egg sandwiches. The car filled up with a greasy smell, but they couldn't care less – they'd been in this car for over two hours; it was time to change anyway.

'Let's try to stick to white cars, Maruti 800s preferably,' Bipin recommended.

'Sure, they shouldn't be difficult to find.'

The Maruti 800 was one of the largest-selling cars in India, and white was the most popular colour in cars. A white Maruti 800 blended into the background easily. Everyone had seen one a couple of million times, and no one gave it a second glance on the road.

The van-driver's shift commenced at eight.

Anuj drove behind the RealStores cash van as it collected the cash from the first three stores. It didn't seem that the driver was taking any detours. Everything was going according to their plan.

09:00 a.m.

As the driver wasn't diverting from the fixed routes, it meant no extra time – barring a traffic jam somewhere, which they couldn't have predicted at any rate. They knew from their reconnaissance journeys that the van with cash would stop next at the RealStores shop in Mayur Vihar Phase I, sometime between 11:30 a.m. and noon. Tailing the driver the entire distance as he collected the moneybags from all the stores made little sense. The fact that the driver had missed their tail on the previous occasions did not guarantee he'd miss spotting them today. If detected, he might baulk and jeopardize their entire plan. Nevertheless, it was time to change the car. It was risky to drive a stolen car for longer than necessary.

Anuj swung to the next left and let the RealStores van continue straight on its course to the next shop.

They found a Maruti Omni this time. Anuj transferred the toolkit to the Omni and they drove off towards Mayur Vihar.

'This has a lot more space,' Bipin commented, as he looked behind.

'Oh, yes.'

'Let's try to pick these up – the space will come in handy, and it's equally ubiquitous, isn't it?'

'You got it, buddy.'

11:15 a.m.

After meandering aimlessly through various sectors in Noida, restricting the number of colas they drank to avoid having to get out of the car to pee, Bipin and Anuj finally reached Mayur Vihar. They drove around the block to check out the available cars. If the car was still parked, it was safe to assume the owner had used some other mode of conveyance to get to work or didn't require it for the day, which lowered the odds of it being reported missing quickly. Anuj picked up another identical white Omni from another block and the two sat patiently in the customer parking outside RealStores.

'Let's hope all goes according to plan.'

'Whatever will be will be …' Bipin responded, gazing heavenwards. Somehow, he didn't find it funny to seek divine intervention in the ungodly quest they had intended to carry out. 'All the best to both of us.'

11:39 a.m.

The white Tata 407 they'd been waiting all morning for, finally swerved into the car park. It took a U-turn in the parking lot and parked three cars away from Bipin and Anuj's Omni. The driver, after getting out, stretched, and sauntered towards the back entrance of the shop where the cargo awaited him. It would take him a minimum of seven minutes – they had timed his absence on previous occasions.

'Good luck!' Bipin whispered as Anuj, waiting with heavy-duty clippers, got out of the Omni and discreetly bent down between the van and the Maruti Esteem parked next to it, disappearing beneath the van.

Bipin looked at the digital clock on the dash. It had been over six minutes since the driver had gone out. Time was running at twice its usual pace it seemed, the green digits were certainly skipping …

... 6 minutes and 10 seconds ...

... 12 ...

... 15 ...

... 19 ...

... 24 ...

... 30 ...

... 36 ...

He saw the van driver walk back with the small plastic bag like he was carrying groceries purchased from the back of the store.

Shit! Where was Anuj?

Bipin thought of walking up to the driver to ask for directions to some place – or something frivolous, just anything – to delay his approach, but decided against it at the last minute. It would be foolish because if he stopped and spoke to the driver, he'd have to get close, and the driver might recognize him later when they approached him on the bridge. No, he couldn't afford that risk. If he got out now, they'd have to abandon the plan altogether.

The driver walked straight to the back of the van.

There were still no signs of Anuj! Had he slipped out from the other side? Perhaps he had crumbled under pressure and abandoned their plan?

Oh god!

Bipin felt his pulse racing, beads of sweat breaking on his forehead, heart pounding like Max Roach's drums; adrenaline rushed through his veins. His hands trembled.

Would their plan fall apart even before it had started? What if the driver had spotted Anuj? He'd surely call the police.

He saw the driver open one of the rear doors, hastily throw the plastic bag in, and lock it, turning the key twice. Double locked and secure for the journey to Connaught Place. The man moved towards the cab in front and, once he got in, took out a diary and made a note, like he was filling in a log.

Suddenly, the driver's door of the Omni opened. Anuj was back from the other side. Smiling.

Mission accomplished! Thank god!

'What happened?' he asked as soon as Anuj got into the driver's seat.

'The van driver was back before I could slip out.'

'So how did you get out? Did he see you?' Bipin was still hyperventilating.

'Take your finger off the panic button, my friend, he didn't see me. He doesn't have wing mirrors, and there's no way he could see me roll out from under the van after he was inside. I slipped away on the other side and walked behind the cars till here.'

'Did you manage to—'

'Yes, I've punctured one of the pipes as we agreed. The brake fluid has already started leaking; there will be a stain underneath as he drives away, but he won't know.' Anuj smiled. 'I reckon he should notice that his brakes are underperforming within five-to-six minutes, so he should – fingers crossed – stop somewhere on the Nizamuddin Bridge as per our plan.'

'Good. Let's move.' Bipin gestured to Anuj as the van started to roll out of the car park.

Their clock had started.

Anuj pulled away slowly and eased in behind the van. As soon as they hit the main road, he'd let a couple of cars get in-between both the vehicles. There was no need to attract attention by speeding or any sort of reckless driving while tailing the van at close quarters. They were just commuters in another vehicle on the road; if they made any errors, people might be able to recall later: *'Oh, yes, there was a white Maruti Omni speeding and zigzagging through the traffic ...'*

'Stay calm, stay normal.'

'It's easy to say that,' Anuj responded with a smile. He raised his left palm for a high-five.

'Best of luck for our mission, buddy.'

The next fifteen to twenty minutes would be crucial to the plan. If they could strictly adhere to it, success was imminent.

22

FREE BIRDS

11:51 a.m.

Bipin and Anuj followed the money van at a distance. Not too close, but never out of sight, not even for a second. They let a car slip between the van and themselves, but later eased back and slowed down to let a few more overtake them. It would be too much of a coincidence if your van broke down on a bridge and the next vehicle that came across happened to be a mechanic's. Even a dumb monkey would smell a rat there.

'He's stalling,' Anuj gestured towards the van in front. They had driven almost two and a half kilometres over the bridge.

'Oh, yeah!'

The van was visibly slowing down and gently veering towards the left to get off the road and onto the unpaved side. Some cars kissing the rear end of the van must have sighted the blinkers late; a horn blew, then a few more.

'It was good to stay a little further away,' Anuj said calmly. He slowed down as they approached the van. Sliding the Omni down from the tarmac, he stopped and idled once their front seat was parallel to the van's.

'What happened?' Bipin rolled down the window and asked.

'The bloody brakes, they aren't responding,' the driver replied. 'Do you know a mechanic nearby?'

'He's one,' Bipin pointed towards Anuj.

'Hmm ...' The driver got down from the van and peeked into the Omni.

'What's wrong?' Anuj asked earnestly. 'When you say the brakes are not responding, do you mean they're loose or are they not working at all?'

'The brakes aren't responding to the pedal. Something's broken.'

'Want me to look?'

'Do you think you can fix it?'

'Not without looking at it.'

'How much?' The driver wanted to know what it would cost him. And he wasn't wrong. Roadside mechanics that turned up at the opportune time could be a rip off. He didn't want to be taken advantage of due to his desperation.

'One hundred,' Anuj told him.

'That's way too much. How about fifty?'

Anuj looked at Bipin like he was sincerely asking for the other mechanic's opinion on price.

'Okay.'

'But only if you can fix it,' the driver of the van clarified. 'It does me no good to know what the fault is and still be stranded out here.'

They didn't need the hundred or the fifty but stopping in the middle of a road to help a stranger without haggling could certainly raise suspicion.

'Twenty if I can't fix it. After all, I'm still putting in my time and labour, it's only fair.'

The driver thought for a second. Perhaps he was pondering if he could explain the expense to his employers. 'Okay then.'

Anuj reversed and parked the Omni right behind the money van and both of them got down. Anuj carried the tool kit. Bipin carried the concealed Diwali pistol. It was time for the rubber to meet the road.

By the time the duo walked up to the van, the driver was craning his neck under the bonnet. 'Fuck! The brake fluid has less than halved, it must have leaked.'

Anuj walked to the left of the van – away from the traffic – and bent down to have a look. 'You're correct. One of the lines is leaking … I can see the oil dripping, but it's a small leak so we still have time.'

'Can you fix it?'

'Yeah.'

'Here?' The driver looked surprised. 'You hardly have tools.'

'I can't fix it totally, but I can repair it enough so that you can drive to your destination slowly. Does that work for you?'

'Anything will. Just fix it however you can please so I can drive it.'

Anuj gave Bipin a quick glance – *Ready, partner?* – and opened his small toolkit.

'How would you do it?' the driver wanted to know.

'You want me to tell you how, so that you can do it yourself and not pay me?' Anuj joked.

'No, just so I know what to do if it ever happens again.'

'It's quite simple. The brake fluid travels to all four wheels. One of the pipes has a leak – maybe some sharp stone hit it without you realizing – so I'll cut that line and plug it with a nail. You can still drive the van with brakes working on three wheels. However, when you apply the brakes, the car will swerve to one side, depending on which of the pipe is cut off. I'll go check now.'

'That's smart.'

'That's what you're paying me the big bucks for.'

'Where's your garage?' the driver asked Bipin when Anuj slipped under the van.

'What?'

'Where is your garage? I mean do you work for a garage or do you two own one?'

'Oh.' Bipin replied, trying to come up with a believable response. Saying GK would not be a smart response. So he went with: 'Gurgaon.'

'That's way off; what are you doing in this part of the city?' The driver asked, bending down to see how Anuj was doing.

Bipin saw the opportunity. He gripped the barrel of his pistol and hit the driver hard on his shoulder. The shoulder was a safe bet; they didn't want to end up in more trouble by gravely injuring the guy. The driver, already squatting, fell prone on his stomach.

'What the fuck—'

Bipin was holding the gun with its nozzle pointed towards the driver. 'One more word and I'll blow your brains out.'

Before the driver could grasp what was happening, Anuj sneaked out and muzzled the driver's mouth with a greased towel. Not that anyone could have heard him yell with the noisy traffic on the other side.

'Keys?' Bipin stretched his hand.

The driver, visibly terrified by the pistol in the old man's hand, shook his head. *No.*

'Keys. I swear I won't ask again, I'll shoot you in the head and take the keys anyway.'

Anuj punched him again, hard on his collarbone this time.

Bipin bent down – keeping his gun hand at a distance from the driver's arm length – and patted him down. The keys were in his right-side trouser pocket. He gestured to Anuj, who slid his hand in, pulled them out and threw them for Bipin to catch. Then, using cable ties, he tied the driver's hands and legs.

Bipin opened the rear of the van, relieved they had changed the plan at the last minute. Transferring so many bags from the van to the Omni would have taken them a long time, especially with one of them busy keeping the driver under control. Although they were still concealed from the road by the parked van, someone could stop to offer help or a police car could drive by. Any minute they could be found out. The only way their plan could work was if they drove away in the stolen van.

'Anuj, how long will it take to fix the van?'

'Two minutes, but we won't be able to drive fast.'

'That's OK, then let's do that.' Bipin didn't question his friend's judgement.

12:11 a.m.

They had to cruise gently at 20 kmph; the speed was ideal in the circumstances. The van swung a hard left every time the brakes were applied, but fortunately Anuj had been able to restore the braking to about seventy percent, so it wasn't so bad. He was alone in the cab in front; Bipin and the driver were in the rear with the money. They were still in their disguises, so it was advisable to adhere to all traffic rules. It would be deeply ironic if they got pulled over for a traffic offence after succeeding in the most difficult phase of their plot.

They had left the Maruti Omni on the roadside with the key in the ignition. Who cared?

12:44 a.m.

The Delhi Zoo, which sprawls across 176 acres of land near the Purana Qila (Old Fort) was established in the late fifties. Rechristened as the National Zoological Park in 1982, it boasted over thirteen-hundred animals in over a hundred species. With Asiatic and Gir lions, royal Bengal tigers, African wild buffaloes, Indian rhinoceros, brow-antlered deer, and chimpanzees, the zoo brought in a constant flow of visitors in their vehicles. What could be a better location for the next step of their plan?

Anuj drove into the car park that was bustling with people and cars.

'Ten rupees,' the parking attendant asked at the barricade.

Anuj paid and drove in. He drove around until he found an empty slot behind a Maruti Omni. He reversed the van into the slot such that the van and the Omni's rears faced each other. He got out, looked around for a few seconds, then quickly picked the Omni's lock and raised its rear hatch-door so that the van's driver inside couldn't note the registration number when they opened the van's doors. With the Omni's rear hatch up and the money-van's rear doors open, there was little anyone could see from the sides.

It was tricky to transfer thirty-five bags of cash while keeping the van's captive driver in check, but after twenty minutes they were done.

'What about him?' Anuj asked as they got out of the van leaving the driver inside.

'Let's leave him inside with this door bolted, not locked. His limbs are tied so he'll need at least ten minutes to roll or crawl to the rear door. Then someone has to be close enough in this noisy place to hear the banging and open it for him. We should be far away by then.'

'We cannot change the van again. Moving all this,' Anuj pointed to the bags inside, 'so let's go.'

'Don't take off the disguise yet.' Bipin winked.

The two got into the Omni and drove away. The parking attendant looked up at the departing vehicle, and stared at Anuj. *Had he recognized Anuj?*

If he did, he did not care. He let them through.

'Holy shit!'

'We made it.'

23

FREE BIRDS

Delhi Zoo

01:00 p.m.

A FAMILY OF FOUR WERE THE FIRST PEOPLE TO HEAR someone kicking and grunting inside a nondescript parked van. They were apprehensive initially, but the man, leaving his wife and two kids where they were, walked closer as he could also hear muffled cries.

Suspicious of a trap, he raised an alarm and knots of people gathered around the van in no time.

Rajendra, the van driver, was finally rescued. Crying, screaming and hyperventilating, he could hardly speak. 'They … have gun … robbed me … mechanic … cash … police.'

Someone in the crowd gave him water. Another person rushed to the parking attendant. Eventually, the police were called.

Near IFFCO Building

01:04 p.m.

'We've covered a good distance,' Anuj said when he spotted the IFFCO building. 'We should be safe now.'

'Yes, even if the driver was rescued five minutes after we left and raised an alarm and got the entire police force in action, what could he tell them about us – an old and a young man in a white Omni? Good luck with that! And in any case, we are out of Delhi Police's jurisdiction.' Bipin thumped Anuj's back in celebration.

Delhi Zoo

01:23 p.m.

The public had untied Rajendra, given him two Brufen tablets and a bottle of Bisleri. They had also checked his neck and hands for any injuries but besides some swelling, the man had not been physically hurt. His assailants seemed to be professionals who had been careful not to hurt him badly.

'What happened?' asked someone in the crowd.

Rajendra narrated his tale of woe in a choking voice. He was still scared out of his wits.

A Delhi Police Gypsy that had been in the vicinity arrived at the scene with two policemen on board: a constable driver who was built like a twig, lean and gangly; his moustache seemed to be the heaviest part of his body and a heavy, thickset sub-inspector who looked like he had eaten his and the constable's dinner.

'What happened here?' the sub-inspector enquired.

Rajendra repeated his despondent story, slow and staccato. How his van had broken down, the two harmless-looking mechanics offering to help him, the pistol … 'Could I make a call?' he requested when he finished.

'To whom?' asked the sub-inspector.

'My employers.'

'Who are they?'

'Mr Harsh Singhal's office.'

'You mean *the* Mr Singhal?'

The Singhal family was well known – old money at the highest rungs of power in Delhi.

'Okay, did you notice anything that could help us in the investigation?'

'An old man, maybe forty-five or fifty with thick dark glasses, and the other one was younger, but he wore one of those long-peaked caps which shaded most of his face …'

'Which vehicle were they in?'

'A white Maruti Omni.'

'Registration number or anything specific on the vehicle – any decals or marks?'

'No.'

A white Maruti Omni in Delhi and surrounding areas with no registration number? It was akin to looking for a particular piece of hay in a haystack.

'Who called us?' the sub-inspector turned and asked the crowd that had grown since the arrival of the police.

'Me.' Someone pointed to their expensive cellular phone.

'Give your phone to Mr Rajendra, he needs to make an urgent call.'

House A 1065, Sector 4, Gurgaon

03:10 p.m.

The safe house Bipin and Anuj had rented in November was near the Old Railway Road. The two had been mindful to change their vehicle one last time. They debated if it was necessary but in the end, agreed it was important to be cautious. The van driver they had left tied up in the Delhi Zoo would certainly tell the police that the two men who robbed him were in a white Maruti Omni. It was best to abandon the vehicle.

They drove into the house in a steel-grey Ford Ikon, closed the gate and emptied the car.

'I'll go and drop this car off somewhere,' Anuj suggested.

'Good idea, but leave after we've taken off the disguises, and changed into something clean. We shouldn't let anyone see you outside with all the grease, just in case the driver has told the police that two motor mechanics had stopped to help him. And when you return, please take a taxi, but get down at the Jai Cinema on the other side, outside Sector 17, and walk back here.'

'I always knew you were smart.'

Bipin smiled.

Delhi Zoo

03:59 p.m.

The crowd had dispersed by now. The constable stood next to Rajendra and the sub-inspector sat in the Gypsy talking on the radio to his boss. The details of the robbery had been taken down, but no case had been filed yet. The bureaucratic machinery was more concerned about who should handle the case: UP Police or Delhi Police? The merchandise stolen had belonged to stores in Noida, but the vehicle had been recovered in Delhi. The victim and sole witness, Rajendra, had clammed up after his initial account and his subsequent call to Mr Singhal's office. He even refused to divulge the amount robbed from his van. All he relayed was that Mr Singhal's team was on its way, and they'd be the ones talking to the police.

House A 1065, Sector 4, Gurgaon

Almost midnight

Anuj had returned to the house at 4:30 p.m. after dropping off the stolen Ford as planned. With the television running in the background to catch any local news on the heist, they sat down to count their loot. It took the two of them over seven hours since the currency was, as expected, in various denominations.

1,14,57366.00

'One crore, fourteen lakhs, and fifty thousand, oh, my god!!

'What about the seven-thousand, three-hundred and sixty-six rupees …?' Bipin called out.

'We'll use that to buy some expensive Scotch and champagne to celebrate the next few days, what do you say?'

'No. We decided not to splurge for the time being. We can't use this currency for anything.'

'But you said the currency won't be marked, how will anyone know?'

'I said that I didn't know that for sure, remember? If the currency is marked indeed, the news will definitely leak out. Let's be patient until we know it isn't. I have some money in my account; I'll go and buy the drinks, but let's not spend this cash for now, okay?

'As long as we can afford to drink something good, it doesn't matter. We've waited all our lives; we can wait a few more days.'

'How many days did you take off work from Munna ji's garage?'

'A week. And you?'

'Same. So no one's going to miss us.'

'What should we do with these bags?' Anuj asked.

'We have to destroy them soon but not immediately. The police might have their description on the record. Maybe we'll burn them later.'

'You've thought about everything.'

For a split second, they both stared at each other; after months and months of planning, they had somehow managed to pull this plan off.

———

Tuesday, 14 January 1997

09:00 a.m.

The two friends watched the news anxiously the next morning. The only news covered on local channels was the daylight heist on the Nizamuddin Bridge.

There was a media storm and, according to the press, the police had no clues. It seemed to Anuj and Bipin that the chips had finally fallen in their favour.

They were hardly surprised the amount of money stolen was reported as around fifty lakhs – less than half the amount they had in the house.

'I told you: they sent cash to the head office to save tax. If they declared the actual sum stolen, the tax authorities would become aware they've been evading taxes all along.'

'So we robbed bigger thieves than us,' Anuj clapped his hands in jubilation.

'Oh, yes!'

'This calls for a celebration.'

'On one condition …'

'What's that?'

'We drink the Old Monk that we have had for a couple of days, and neither of us goes out after drinking. Not even to make a call to Manasi. Once the alcohol lubricates the tongue, things spill out. We need to be extra vigilant. Deal?'

'Deal. But who goes out to buy Scotch and champagne on—' Anuj tried calculating.

'I'll buy that on Thursday morning. Until then, we eat the food we've already stocked, drink what's in the house, watch television and follow the news.'

'Done.'

They shook hands and hugged.

'Have you considered how you will explain your newfound riches to Manasi?'

'No.'

'Then let's come up with something.'

10:15 a.m.

'I can't find my driving licence,' Anuj said after breakfast.

'Are you kidding?' Bipin almost yelled.

'I've been looking for it since last evening, but I can't find it anywhere.'

'When did you last see it?'

'I can't remember if I had it in my pocket when we left home yesterday.'

'Why didn't you tell me when we got back?'

'What would you have done then? Called up the police to check if I dropped it in the van?' Anuj smiled.

How could anyone smile in a situation like that? Anuj had always been a bit duh! But this was more than a bit, wasn't it? This was duh-squared! He may have single-handedly ruined their plan.

'That small piece of plastic could land us in serious trouble, Anuj.'

'Take a chill pill, *yaar*. I'm pretty sure it wasn't in my pocket. It must be lying in the barsaati; I'll find it when we get back.'

'Are you sure?'

'I'm not a hundred percent sure, but I'm reasonably confident I didn't drop it anywhere.'

'As long as you didn't drop it in the RealStores van, I doubt the police can connect it to the robbery even if someone finds it and sends it to them.'

'That's spoken like an optimist.'

'Exactly. Remember, the glass should always seem half full.'

24

THE POLICE

A TURF WAR IS GENERALLY DESCRIBED AS AN ACRIMONIOUS dispute between conflicting groups over a geographical territory. On the face of it, this was hardly some turf war, far from it. First off, the two factions in this case – Delhi and Uttar Pradesh Police – weren't exactly rivals; they were just two divisions of the Indian police. Secondly, they weren't fighting over who'd take the lead in the investigation of the daylight heist. Instead, neither wanted to take the responsibility, and fought tooth and nail to stay clear of the high-profile case: *It's not ours. It's theirs.*

In the end, after several hours of bickering and finger-pointing, the music finally stopped with the UP Police holding the baton. Although the van – the site of the robbery and hence, the crime scene – was recovered in Delhi, the capital's police argued that there was no guarantee that the robbers hadn't escaped back to UP or Rajasthan or Haryana so how could the case be registered in their jurisdiction? With crime on the rise and ever-decreasing manpower and budgets, they convinced everyone that since the cash stolen belonged to Uttar Pradesh, it was logical that UP Police should investigate. Of course, they'd extend all assistance – read lip service – wherever required. The UP Police too, if they had a choice in the matter, would have dumped the case to their janitors for all they cared, but Harsh Singhal had several connections high up the chain of command and the pressure cascaded to solve the case quickly.

The investigation finally began after 9 p.m. on Monday, over five hours since the first call from the Delhi Zoo. Rajendra, the injured van driver, had been taken to the Govind Ballabh Pant Hospital at JLN Marg, so they paid a visit to him first, but Rajendra had nothing new to add. If anything, he had further clammed up after Mr Singhal's men had intervened and started exerting pressure on the police machinery.

From whatever the UP Police had gathered so far, logic dictated inside knowledge, since the Singhal team had reiterated that no one outside of their business associates knew about the clandestine biweekly operation that had run for over a decade now. All employees who had knowledge of the operation obviously had alibis, since they were manning the stores at the time of the heist. Of course, they could have inadvertently shared the information with outsiders, but all the employees only had partial knowledge about the operation. No one questioned by the police knew the details of the route the van took, the order in which stores were visited, the timings and other details, except the driver, Rajendra himself. The driver too was vouched for by his employers and not found to have any associates that could have committed the crime.

The van recovered from Delhi Zoo was transported back to Noida and stripped bare, but the forensics found zilch. The perpetrators had worn gloves at all times, and covered their heads too, it seemed. The van, on the other hand, was full of prints and DNA from scores of people who emptied the cargo in Delhi. It was virtually impossible to keep track of whom to include or eliminate since the personnel had changed several times in the last ten years or so.

The UP Police strongly believed – using their shrewd detective skills – that the job was carried out by a gang of professional robbers. It had all the hallmarks: a heist in broad daylight in an area where the traffic hardly had a dull moment who else could have immaculately planned and made away with half-a-crore rupees with such precision? No amateur would start this big and so audaciously. Anyone new would start with a few small jobs, and build up their skills and confidence first. And with that one wrong hypothesis, the UP Police went off the rails. Their wrong assumption distracted them and they had erred in the most classic way: they started to fit the facts to their theory.

And so, all known offenders in and around Noida were brought in for questioning, and grilled and only let off after their innocence was confirmed with credence. Heat was turned up on the snitches in the locality, but they too came up empty-handed. There had been no rumours to dig further into.

The alibis of all history-sheeters, everyone with a record of break-ins, robberies, assaults, and similar accusations, were checked and rechecked. Still nothing. It was reasoned that the two professionals had travelled from some other state with the specific target in mind, raided the van and bolted. The UP Police believed – at least they desperately wanted to – that the miscreants were from another state. Messages were relayed to neighbouring states of Haryana, Rajasthan, even Madhya Pradesh to look for known criminals that operated in twos: an old-and-young-man team.

The currency, because it was taken from the checkout tills, wasn't marked.

The van driver had mentioned that the thieves had carried a pistol. He couldn't provide any description of the weapon except that it was a '*kaale rang ki bandook*', a black pistol. All known illegal-weapon dealers were contacted to check if such a handgun had been sold recently. Nada.

The UP Police jumped from one pointless idea to another, one false lead to the next until they ran out of ideas and exhausted all leads. All their theories had toppled and crashed. What next?

They caught a lucky break on 14 January around 9:30 a.m. The white Maruti Omni, which was reported stolen from Delhi Zoo around the same time as the robbers' disappearance, was found abandoned in Gurgaon. It wasn't that the two criminals had left the Omni with their forwarding address taped to the steering wheel. But it gave the UP Police an excuse to get the monkey off their backs. They reasoned, however weakly, that it was plausible, to move the investigation to Gurgaon Police, since the vehicle was found in a different state. First, they convinced themselves that the thieves were holed up somewhere in Gurgaon, and then they persuaded Mr Harsh Singhal's team to ask the Gurgaon Police to take charge of the case. Of course, they'd extend all assistance …!

Tired of the police politics, Mr Singhal turned up at the Gurgaon's Police Commissionerate to personally meet Commissioner Raj Mehra.

No appointment was required. The Singhal family was extremely influential. Anyone who owned businesses that turned over that kind of money had to be. The reverse was also true: only an influential family made that kind of money. However one wanted to see it, the truth was that the family was connected to the highest echelons of power. It was in fact a sign of humility that they had approached the Gurgaon Police Commissioner for help, and not called the home minister directly. The pressure to help the family, of course, was immense. Commissioner Mehra assured Harsh Singhal that he'd do whatever he could to bring the criminals to justice. Then he called his deputy to put together a team and get into action without further delay.

As is typical of such cases, the pressure exponentially

increases as it travels downwards; maybe gravity increases its speed and intensity. Senior Inspector Arfan 'Arfy' Khan was about to chair a departmental meeting of his team when his superior called to hand him a new case. His boss explained the facts, the precarious circumstances of the robbery, and told him to head the task force. In truth, the high-profile case did not have any leads and the department was readying a scapegoat in light of the media scrutiny.

'Thank you for showing confidence in me, sir,' Arfy said, scribbling the details on a notepad.

'Drop everything and investigate this first. Give me a call if you need any extra resources or cooperation from other police departments. The commissioner and I are looking for quick results.'

'I'll do my best, sir—'

The line had already disconnected.

25

JAILBIRDS

ARFY RETURNED TO THE INTERROGATION ROOM AND sat down wordlessly. He looked at Bipin and smiled victoriously; he had, after all, won as Bipin had sent the slip through Sharma that he was ready to talk, turn into a state witness and, most importantly, provide the location where the cash was hidden.

But before he could say something, there was a soft knock on the door. Constable Bhim Singh walked in with coffees, looking miserable. Did they not have anyone else in this police station with a happier disposition?

So, Arfy had ordered coffees before coming in.

Was it his final visit? This was it? Was their little caper over?

Bhim Singh, glaring at Bipin, carried a severely dented and blackened handolium kettle, and freshly washed glasses stacked on top of each other, many of which appeared to be still shedding drops of water. He poured the coffee into three glasses, looking at Arfy for further instructions.

'Give his buddy two coffees …' Arfy pointed at Bipin, '… and that lawyer in the other room. Tell them I'll be with them soon, in twenty minutes or so.'

'But, sir—'

'What?'

'These coffees already have sugar in them.'

'Oh, thanks for reminding me. Get another one without sugar for the lawyer. We don't want to get a lawyer's glucose level up. The lawyers across the city will skin us alive. They'd claim we did it deliberately and charge us for manslaughter.' He looked at Sharma and grinned.

'Yes, sir.'

Shit!

Bipin glanced at Sharma and figured that his lawyer, too, would be thinking along similar lines. If he had worked it out, so would have Sharma. If only they had another day. With his two careless comments over the past two visits, Arfy had practically given away Anuj's lawyer's identity. First: she was a woman. Second: she was diabetic, or at the very least she had high blood sugar. The pool of diabetic women working as public defenders would be simple to navigate. But alas, they had run out of time. Today was it. There was little point in attacking the opponent's king after you've already been checkmated. They had no more moves left, it seemed.

If Arfy was planning a final chat with Anuj and his lawyer soon after, could Bipin afford to take a last-minute risk? The anxiety, the uncertainty gnawed at him. Would Anuj and his lawyer know that the net cast by Bipin's lawyer was about to yield results? Would Anuj hold back?

'Have you guys heard the fable of the tortoise and the scorpion? Wait, I think it was a frog, not a tortoise ...'

Neither Bipin nor his lawyer had the stomach to listen to the inspector's pointless stories but they did not have the balls to tell him to shut up either.

'Yes, I'm quite sure it was a frog,' Arfy carried on, oblivious to his audience's impassive reaction. 'So, on one stormy day a scorpion asked a frog to carry it across the river. Naturally the frog hesitated, as he knew that the scorpion could sting him. But the scorpion claimed that it would not sting the frog because if it did so, they would both drown, and why would the scorpion want that?' Arfy paused. 'Do you guys follow the scorpion's logic?' he asked both, but looked squarely at Bipin.

'Yes.' *And now could you just complete your bloody story and come to the point? God, this inspector was a piece of work!*

'So the frog did. He was sold on the scorpion's logic like you, and he agreed to carry the scorpion. However, halfway across the river, the scorpion stung the frog. "Why did you do that?" asked the frog in pain. "Now we will both die." And do you know what the scorpion said in response?' Arfy paused again and looked from Bipin to Sharma and back to Bipin and waited for a response. When none came he continued to fill in the blanks. 'The scorpion said, "I know, but it's in my nature to do so." You see, you can change anything but not a person's inherent nature.' Arfy looked Bipin in the eye as though he was trying to pass on some hint with the fable he'd just narrated.

Despite knowing that the inspector was provoking him, it still made Bipin brood: Anuj knew Bipin had once loved Manasi. Anuj would feel jealous. Anuj was hot-headed – it was in his nature to lose his temper, wasn't it? Was the inspector suggesting something?

'So … you said, your client wants to talk, Mr Sharma?' Arfy took a noisy slurp and segued the conversation earnestly, as though he hadn't just wasted the last ten minutes on a needless story.

'And also negotiate the terms and conditions before he tells you anything,' Sharma pointed out.

'Oh, yes, so what does sonny boy want in exchange?'

'Could you please ask your team to switch off the recording, so that whatever we say before my client gives his statement is off the record please?'

'OK.' Arfy got up and went out for a second. He returned and a few seconds later, turned off the red light. 'So, off the record, let's hear what sonny boy wants?'

'My client Bipin Desai wants a full pardon in exchange for the information he provides.'

'And does he want Angelina Jolie along with it or Jennifer Aniston or both?'

'What do you mean?'

'I'm sure he also wants a threesome when he gets a full pardon, so I thought I'd propose some names.' Arfy shook his head. 'Mr Sharma, this isn't a roadside masala fish cart where we serve clients, and sonny boy here wants extra salt and pepper on his chips. You're wasting your time and mine. I thought you guys had reached a sensible decision before you asked me to leave the other group halfway through a serious discussion and come here to listen to this tripe. A full pardon is out of the question. It's not going to happen.'

'What is your offer then?'

'When we file the charges to the court, I can ask the prosecutor to show some leniency towards sonny boy here on account of his cooperation, but only if he divulges where the loot is and turns into a state witness against his friend. I will ask the prosecution to take a year off his total sentence for being a co-conspirator. Like I said, I have to be fair, and I said the same to Atul or Anup or whatever his friend's name is. Nothing more, nothing less – I hope I have made myself very clear.'

'That's not enough—' Sharma started.

'Take it or leave it.' Arfy got up. 'And please do not disturb me again if you come up with another equally ludicrous proposal. You're a man of the world, Mr Sharma. Think about it: Have you ever heard of a total pardon in such cases? The prosecutor will kick me hard in my balls if

I even ask for it.' Arfy looked down at his crotch to stress the point.

'Okay, wait.' Sharma stood up and politely gestured to Arfy to take his seat. Almost pleading. 'Just wait a minute, sir ...'

'So you have already thought of something better, and were just trying your luck, testing me to see if you can bluff me? Let me warn you that I'm not amused by your tactics, Mr Sharma. I expected mature behaviour.'

'No, sir, I'm extremely sorry, but please give us a hint about what you have in mind, sir.'

'I told you: one year less than the other one. OK, I'll take two years off from the prison time. Does that work for your client?'

'Half.' Sharma glanced at Bipin who sat stoically. Sharma had already prepared him for this so there was no reason to object now.

'Half what?'

'If my client divulges all the information you require to prosecute his accomplice, then you will speak to the prosecutor to slash his prison sentence by half,' Sharma explained.

'There's no way the prosecutor is going to agree to it, I can tell you now. He'll still kick my balls.' Arfy focused on his crotch again.

Comedian number one!

'But Bipin will lead you to the cash; he'll testify against his own friend, and you will have an iron-clad case.'

'It's still too much to ask for, considering his crime.'

'It's his first mischief—'

'Mischief … you describe his crime as mischief, Mr Sharma? They looted more than fifty lakhs, carried an unlicenced firearm, injured the driver and stole multiple cars … some mischief that was. For god's sake, it wasn't even a spur-of-the-moment crime; it was a planned heist. The driver could have died!'

He didn't die though. I was very careful when I hit him so as to not hurt him, you liar, Bipin wanted to yell but it would be unwise to admit to anything yet.

'I'm sorry, I didn't mean that. I meant it's his first offence, sir, and he got carried away. But now he regrets it and is willing to cooperate. You can grant him a second chance, SI Khan … please.' Almost begging now.

'You think it was mischief, Bimal Desai?'

'No, sir, but I'm really and truly sorry. I promise you I will never do anything stupid like this ever again.' Bipin's voice sounded like it came from the bottom of a hundred-foot well. He had done well not letting the tears flow, but maybe if he had let them flow, the plea may have worked better on the inspector. He noticed that his left hand had been incessantly tapping his left leg. Anxiety. Fear. Uncertainty.

'Of course you won't. The police will have you on record. One more mistake and you will be in so much shit that even God won't be able to pull you out of the sewer next time around, do you understand?'

Bipin nodded. He had been reckless once, but he understood the repercussions of attempting anything like this again. The first-time offender excuse by definition couldn't work the second time. Anyway, if he testified against his friend and got a lighter sentence in lieu, even when Anuj got out of prison, he would never talk to Bipin again. Then, who would Bipin have left in the world to ever plan anything like this with? He could bet Manasi wouldn't speak to him after this, either. They had made a terrible blunder; now their friendship would be over, their little family broken. Manasi would never forgive him. He'd have to leave town, go elsewhere ... God, why had he been so irresponsible? A decent job, and a barsaati to live in ... he could have grown in the corporate world ...

'Okay, I'll ask the prosecutor for a reduction in our sonny boy's prison time by fifty percent.'

Sharma looked at Bipin for the final approval.

Bipin acquiesced with a nod. 'Thank you, sir.'

'Good, now let's get the recording started.'

Arfy knocked on the door twice in quick succession, and waited. The red light came on after a few seconds – some kind of a code.

'So where would you like to begin? I want the whole nine yards not a precis, and don't lie, not even by omission.' he looked at Bipin. 'We're ready when you are, sonny boy ...'

Bipin told SI Arfy Khan the whole story from the beginning with the camera on. Everything from the time they had started planning the heist, the recon trips, the fake gun, the leaking brake-fluid line. Arfy sat amused, smiling and expressing surprise at a few points in the narrative. After fifteen minutes of non-stop talking, Bipin was through the entire thing.

'You must feel lighter now,' Arfy said. 'Confession, they say, is good for the soul, the truth will set you free, Bansi Desai.'

Bipin nodded simply. What was left to say now? Once in jail, his identity would be a mere number. Bansi or Bipin didn't matter anymore, did it?

'How much cash did you guys get away with?'

Bipin knew that the media had claimed something like fifty lakhs, but was there any point in lying now? When Arfy went into the house in Gurgaon he'd find all of it anyway. If only they had hidden half of it elsewhere.

'One crore and fourteen lakhs plus change.'

'I knew it.' Arfy banged his fist loudly on the table. 'I knew the Singhals were cooking their books, skimming money from the top to dodge taxes. Bloody hypocrites, robbing the government; how ironical that it isn't theft when the rich steal from the government, but when you rob the rich, it is theft. But that's the law, isn't it?'

Bipin sat quietly, resigned to his fate.

'Now tell me where you hid the money, sonny boy.'

Bipin wanted to cry.

No, he wanted to weep.

26

THE POLICE

THE MOST POWERFUL CARD IN THE PACK IS NOT AN ACE; it's the joker.

There are 206 bones in an adult human body. Sadly, some folks don't have a single funny one. On the opposite end of that spectrum was Senior Inspector Arfan 'Arfy' Khan, who did not have a single bone that wasn't funny. Clumsy, butter-fingered and yet quick-witted, he bumped into things when he walked, he missed classes in college because he lost track of time, gave sarcastic rejoinders to professors, questioned them, but in the end he still managed to top the class. Soon he recognized his clumsiness had actually put him at an advantage. Sometimes, he pretended to be awkward and clownish only to make people around him laugh. He had taken the cliché *laughter is the best medicine* to heart. It wasn't enough for others to laugh with him or at him, he had realized early in life that it also opened doors, started conversations,

put people at ease while talking to him. He deliberately
faltered for people to fill in the gaps, addressed people
with incorrect names for them to correct, thereby taking
him as an absent-minded fool; if they thought he was a
buffoon, they grew confident, opened up, loosened their
tongues. He was impossible to read on short acquaintance;
it was indiscernible when he tumbled for real or when he
orchestrated the clumsiness. Sometimes, even those close
to him, who knew that he intentionally indulged in such
tomfoolery at times, couldn't determine if it was genuine
or a facade. Years of practice.

Arfy came from a very rich family in Uttar Pradesh.
His grandfather was a Nawab. The princely state had
been integrated into the Republic of India in 1947, but
the privileges and allowances were given to the ruling
classes. But those privy purses, too, were abolished by the
central government in 1971. Nevertheless, Arfy Khan had
inherited enough wealth to not have to work a single day
in his life. He didn't worry too much if the commissioner
was an asshole. Arfy could walk out any day he wanted –
he didn't need the money, and he didn't need the police
uniform for power. Many of his cousins were leaders
in local municipalities across UP. If he quit, he could
always take up politics as a profession. After all, he was an
erstwhile Nawab.

Everyone who knew Arfy long knew he had a sharp
brain. Except, as in most cases, his boss, the commissioner
of Gurgaon police, Raj Mehra. Commissioner Mehra didn't

like him one bit either, and he didn't mince words when he talked to him or about him: *That fool, that incompetent officer, that idiot is a couple of sandwiches short of a picnic, that joker with room temperature IQ, that nawabzada ...*

Part of the commissioner's dislike also stemmed from the fact that Arfy was one of the most highly educated individuals in Gurgaon Police. Arfy Khan had a doctorate in economics. And in some of the team interactions, Arfy Khan tried to argue a point with the commissioner in public. Talk about putting one's foot in one's mouth, Arfy could never control putting his shoes along with his foot in his rictus. The dislike had metamorphosed into abhorrence in a single afternoon. If the commissioner had his way, he'd suspend Arfy, but the debate – or at least Arfy's unsuccessful attempt – had been expressed respectfully. He had been correct in pointing out the wrong statistic the commissioner had been belting out, and he had been polite. Arfy, despite the chagrin of commissioner, hadn't given Mehra any fodder to sack him or suspend him or even transfer him. Moreover, like all large organizations, Commissioner Mehra had his own nemeses in the constabulary who loved Arfy enough to save his ass.

Then there were other sycophantic police officers, including his contemporaries and seniors, who spent most of their working hours kissing asses of those who, in turn, kissed the asses of the ones above them. A virtual pyramid of servile minions existed in the department bestowing full-service ass-kissing. This was true for all bureaucratic departments, to be honest. Sycophancy could decide fates, if promotion was the sole motive of fate. Self-worth came a distant second. But the fact remained that there were enough ass-kissers milking the system and thereby waltzing to higher positions in life. All aboard the gravy train. It worked for some, but it wouldn't for Arfy. He'd be caught if he dished out insincere praises or expressed admiration where it wasn't due. The only thing worse than not kissing ass was to be caught off the mark when kissing ass. Although it was all a facade for career advancement and prime positions in the constabulary, the pretence couldn't be obvious. Only pretension that resembled earnestness got rewarded.

Arfy always found it hilarious that people worked hard to avoid work. And it worked for them. To each his own, he thought. But for now, the spotlight was fixed on him. He couldn't afford to fail under the eye of the commissioner who despised him; it would be a disaster for his career.

Correction: it would be the end of his career. And the commissioner would be delighted to drive the final nail into Arfy personally.

27

THE POLICE

Tuesday, 14 January 1997

22 hours after the heist

THE FIRST TWENTY-FOUR HOURS FOLLOWING A CRIME, whether it's a case of murder or otherwise, are pivotal. But, poor Arfy had received charge of the case around ten in the morning, twenty hours post the crime. To make matters worse, the notes handed over by the UP Police were worthless. After all, if they had any value, the UP Police would have caught the perpetrators themselves by now.

But it was what it was.

Losing twenty hours meant that the perpetrators could have flown to the other end of the world, although unlikely since flying anywhere with such a huge amount of cash was impossible. Yes, they could have transferred the money through hawala and fled the country. Even if the amount declared by Harsh Singhal was correct – which

Arfy did not believe for a second – the suspects could have afforded premium rates to transfer the money and fled. But something in his gut told him that was implausible. The news of the robbery had broken within an hour of their escape. It would have been impossible to arrange a hawala in an hour. And it would be extremely difficult to arrange one after the news had broken out; hawala brokers would not want to be involved in stolen cash. They had rules in illegal businesses too. That said, twenty-two hours of non-stop driving from Delhi could get them into Mumbai or anywhere else in the country.

Arfy, his team of four inspectors and their underlings had a meeting at the Sadar Police Station at 10:30 a.m. Strong coffee was served to wake up anyone who had had a long shift the previous evening. If you had a hangover, tough luck! The briefing was short and to the point: the various tasks were being split between the teams and the investigation began immediately. Everyone was asked to follow every lead, however tenuous the connection. Every contact with someone relevant had to be reported back for another member of the team to look at with fresh eyes. They couldn't afford to miss anything.

As the teams left the police station, Arfy called up his counterparts in Delhi and Noida Police and asked them to send him their latest bulletins on all robberies in the past six months. He wanted to see if any trends had been missed; any similar robberies, any patterns that might emerge. Nothing.

He ordered another pot of black coffee from a nearby vendor. As he sat at his desk with the robbery bulletins spread out in front of him, a particular piece of information stood out: on the day of the robbery – 13 January – there had been an inordinate number of cars stolen. It could have been a sheer coincidence, but what caught his eye was that, in each instance, the stolen car had been discarded in the vicinity of another stolen car on the same day. What were the odds that this was being carried out by different groups of people? Nobody else in the UP Police had made the connection yet. But it became apparent to Arfy that someone had been stealing cars and then swapping them for another one after a few hours like they were trying hard not to be caught in a stolen vehicle. Car thieves stole cars to sell them and make money, not to abandon them. This was something else altogether.

His alarm bells started ringing when he read that a white Maruti Omni with an Uttar Pradesh registration plate that had been stolen from Mayur Vihar Phase 1 had been found abandoned on the Nizamuddin Bridge at the same location where the van driver had stopped the vehicle and had been attacked. How had the UP Police not noticed that? Maybe they were more interested in passing the case on to someone else than investigating it. And they had been successful in doing that. But Arfy couldn't care less. He started calling police stations and working backwards; he realized that the first of the seven cars stolen – a Fiat Uno – was nicked near Greater Kailash early the previous morning. If his hypothesis was correct, there had to be another car stolen around where the suspects had dropped the Omni picked up from the Delhi Zoo, for their forward journey. A Ford Ikon had been reported missing, and it was later recovered from Sector 17 in Gurgaon. Given the amount of baggage – fifty lakh rupees or more – it was improbable that the robbers had dropped the car and taken public transport to carry the cash. Arfy was confident that the suspects had driven to their hiding location in the Ford Ikon first and unloaded it before driving to Sector 17 to abandon the Ford. Then they had either taken public transport to their hidey-hole or walked back. His instinct told him they hadn't gone far, that they were still in the vicinity.

But where?

Arfy requested that all news of the investigation be kept from the media. If the perps were still in Gurgaon, they might get reckless. Reckless was good for the investigation. He was like a bloodhound on the scent. He ordered more manpower. Dozens of plainclothes police personnel were deployed in commercial and residential areas. His reasoning was that the robbers couldn't be holed up for long: they had to come out. But how would the police know whom to watch?

He called the various police stations and sent teams to check all the stolen vehicles that had been recovered. The robbers had been careful to wear gloves and not leave any traces behind, but hopefully they were careless enough to leave some evidence in the stolen vehicle.

24 hours after the heist

One of the search teams got lucky. They found a driving licence of one Mr Anuj Shastri in one of the stolen cars that had been abandoned in Noida and recovered by the police. The UP Police hadn't bothered to search it, and the owner had missed it since licence had slipped under the driver's seat.

Arfy spoke to the owner on the phone, who confirmed that he had never met or known any person by the name of Anuj Shastri. There was no reason for a stranger's driving licence to have found its way into his car.

'Thank you, sir,' Arfy said and disconnected the call.

While piecing together a jigsaw, one often had to fill gaps with phantom pieces: conjectures, hypothesis, logic, instinct, imagination. This could have led to that or that had to be there or if this didn't fit, that would, those kinds of things. *Of course, the person who nicked the car for a brief period accidently dropped it and didn't realize his mistake* was Arfy's surmise for the driving licence discovered in a stolen car. How else did it get there?

That led Arfy to believe this was a rookie job, and Anuj Shastri had to be one of the two men involved. He told his team not to reveal where they had found the licence. When the time came, this information could be useful.

With one of the suspects identified, it was only a matter of time before they identified the other one involved in the heist. Maybe one of them would take the bait, try to correct him and end up confessing their crime.

The address on Anuj Shastri's driving licence was in Greater Kailash. The first car stolen yesterday morning had been picked from the area. It had been recovered from Lajpat Nagar – on the way to Noida. What were the odds that it was someone else and not Mr Anuj Shastri? The pieces of the jigsaw were finally falling into place.

28 hours after the heist

The local police located Mr Rao, the landlord of the address listed on Anuj Shastri's driving licence. He stayed three blocks away and was requested to meet the Senior Inspector on site. He made all the standard excuses people gave to not meet with anyone from the police – '*I hardly know the tenant personally*', '*What's it got to do with me?*'

He was told that Senior Inspector Arfy Khan was on his way from Gurgaon so he better get his fat ass to the barsaati to answer some questions.

Arfy thanked him, put him at ease and asked him about Anuj Shastri.

'I don't know him.' Mr Rao didn't have to look twice at the licence. He was sure.

'Is he not your tenant then?'

'No, sir, my tenant's name is Bipin Desai.' The landlord looked at the licence again and shook his head. 'Not him;

this guy must be a friend of Bipin's but I don't know him. He shouldn't use this address on his driving licence. Before I know, he will start telling people this is his property. These boys, I tell you. When I see Bipin I will tell him this is not acceptable, sir. Don't you think it's wrong behaviour?'

'It is,' Arfy said but his mind was elsewhere. *Bipin Desai,* he repeated in his mind. 'Do you have a duplicate set of keys for the barsaati, Mr Rao?' he asked.

'Of course, but I'm not sure we should enter without permission.'

'Leave the legality to us, Mr Rao. This is a police investigation.'

'Okay.'

There was nothing in the barsaati that could point towards the robbery. However, there were other papers that gave particulars of the two men who stayed here. Bipin Desai, the tenant, worked at a global multinational in Nehru Place, and his partner in crime, Anuj Shastri, worked at a local garage owned by someone called Munna ji.

Munna ji welcomed the police. His initial thoughts were that the police had come to enquire about the land he had occupied illegally. But SI Arfy Khan was keen to know about Anuj, and not about the garage or whose land it was.

'What has he done?' asked Munna ji.

'Oh, nothing. We just want to know about him in connection with another case. He could be a possible witness.'

'Anuj is a good guy, quick learner. He's been a bit unfortunate though—'

'Unfortunate, how?'

'Tea, sir?'

'No, I'm fine.'

'Please, sir, you've come to my garage for the first time.'

'Yes, please then, thanks.' Arfy didn't want the tea, but he reckoned it would make Munna ji feel comfortable.

'Oye, Chhotu,' Munna ji shouted. 'Get a few teas. Full, not half, okay?'

'You were saying something, Munna ji – how is Anuj unfortunate?'

'Oh, his father is a dictator I tell you; threw the young boy out of the house. Even when Manasi got pregnant—'

'Who's Manasi?'

'His wife.'

The tea arrived. It was sweeter than a pudding, but Arfy kept sipping it as he talked. 'So, Anuj is married? Where does his wife live then?' Arfy couldn't imagine Anuj and his wife living with Bipin in the barsaati. In the cursory visual inspection they had made of the barsaati, he hadn't found any women's clothing or toiletries. Or maybe there were some, but not enough to suggest that a woman lived there full-time.

Munna ji, who loved to chat, continued talking and didn't stop until he finished not one but two tea-flavoured puddings. How Anuj and Manasi got married, how he had an accident and lost one of his fingers … 'Manasi has presently gone to her mother's place until the delivery. Have another tea, sir.'

Arfy declined. 'So Bipin and Anuj are good friends,' he asked.

'They're more than friends, they're like brothers. Has he been witness to something serious, Khan-*saab*?'

'Nothing at all. Do you have Manasi's mother's address by any chance?'

'No, but I have Anuj's parents' address. Manasi's and Bipin's parents live in the same colony ...' Munna ji, eager to forge a connection with this important-looking inspector, was a goldmine of information. He obliged Arfy with everything: surnames, families, appearances, mannerisms, habits.

30 hours after the heist

Finding Manasi Upadhaya was child's play in the Munirka DDA Flats, but she was about to go into labour when the police arrived.

'Is everything okay with Anuj? And Bipin? They went to Jaipur ...'

'Yes, nothing to worry about. We were only looking for them since there's been an accident on NH8 that goes from Delhi to Jaipur, and they could be possible witnesses to it,' Arfy explained.

'Okay,' Manasi sighed, with visible relief on her face. A thin smile started to appear.

'Did they say when they were coming back?

'Sunday.'

'By any chance, do you have pictures of Anuj and Bipin?'

'Of course, I have lots of photographs.'

When asked, Manasi also provided two names of their college friends. They hadn't stayed in touch with them though.

Wednesday, 15 January 1997

45 hours after the heist

Bipin's manager, Mr Dixit, a forty-something corporate man with thick glasses and scant hair on his scalp – was equally courteous, although he didn't like the presence of the police in the office premises. Arfy gave the same reason he had given Manasi as to why he was looking for Bipin and his friend.

The manager didn't know Anuj, but obliged the police's request. He asked the HR representative to bring Bipin's file and pulled out his résumé.

If Arfy had any doubts before, Bipin's resume cleared the mist. Before working for this multinational company, Bipin had worked for RealStores in Noida.

The manager provided further tidbits of information that Arfy noted down. Then he left for Gurgaon.

48 hours after the heist

Back at Sadar Police Station, Arfy patched Bipin and Anuj's lives together based on the statements provided by their landlord, their employers and their family members. With every discovery, the picture grew clearer, like another piece of the jigsaw fitting into place. No wonder the two of them had all the inside information required to carry out the heist – Bipin was an ex-employee of RealStores.

In reading his notes on Bipin and Anuj's middle-class upbringing, Arfy was struck by the degree of similarity between their lives. Both their fathers worked in the public sector; their families lived in the DDA flats in Munirka; they went to the same college; and the two lived together after leaving Munirka. If that wasn't enough, one of their old college friends whom Arfy had spoken to on the phone, revealed other details about Manasi, Anuj and Bipin – on how the trio stuck together all the time like they were an item.

Two teams were also sent to Munirka and Greater Kailash and asked not to leave either site even for a second. The instructions were clear: *If both of you need to pee, one of you has to tighten your bladder until the other one has finished his business. If you miss them for any reason, find yourself another job. If you can find one, that is ...*

Certainly rookies, Arfy thought. They had made the rudimentary mistake of underestimating the police.

He called his team for a meeting, circulated photographs of the two perpetrators, and told them to be on high alert. 'Forget everything for the next twenty-four hours ...'

Anuj, the motor mechanic apprentice, did not have any credit or debit cards, but Bipin had both. Arfy called the bank to block both the cards, and inform the police immediately in case he tried using them anywhere in the country. It might be futile since the two men had enough cash, but it was best to try all measures, just in case ...

28

FREE BIRDS

IT HAD BEEN TWO DAYS SINCE THE ROBBERY; BIPIN AND Anuj had been in self-imprisonment in the safe house drinking Old Monk, eating whatever they had in stock – eggs and bread primarily – and watching television.

Fortunately, the police still hadn't discovered relevant clues. The name of the van driver they had robbed was Rajendra, and he had been taken to some hospital. He had described his attackers as an-old-and-a-young-man team. Their disguises had worked. He couldn't define any other feature. No sketches of the robbers had been circulated.

'Attackers?' Anuj exclaimed. 'We hardly attacked him – just a soft whack, that's it.'

The Noida Police was still investigating the case, which was a good thing. The UP Police would surely be looking for them in the wrong places. The police also warned that the two men were armed and dangerous.

'See, he never figured that it was a fake pistol,' Bipin reminded Anuj proudly.

'When do we wrap up from here?'

'Gradually, and in two phases. We should aim to leave in the next few days, maybe Saturday or Sunday so that we're back at work on Monday as planned. Unplanned leave at work might make cause people to take notice and ask questions, so let's not give them a chance. However, we'll leave the cash here and come back for it later. The house is safe, we've already paid rent in advance, so we can come and go anytime we please. We will let the news of the robbery settle down before we look for a way to use the money. We can start by spending a few notes first to see if they are marked before we start celebrating.'

'Hmm ...'

'We act normal like nothing has happened. We feign ignorance, if asked, about a heist on the Nizamuddin Bridge since we were out of town. We were enjoying our little break and not following the Delhi news.'

'Got it,' Anuj agreed.

'We also need to work on our story.'

'What story?'

'Where we went, what we did, which hotel we stayed in – that kind of thing. We can't give people different accounts. The story should be consistent.'

'Yeah, you're right. I never thought about that.'

'I'm glad you agree.'

'But when can we go out to buy Scotch?'

'Tomorrow, definitely.'

'And when can I see Manasi – she might deliver our baby while I am hibernating here.'

'But you have a lifetime to make it up to Manasi with all the money you have now, brother.'

'That's right. But you must get Scotch and champagne tomorrow. I'm dying to celebrate.'

'I promise. But for now, let's finish the Old Monk.'

'But there's no cola left.'

'We have *Seven-Up*.'

'Yuck!'

'Come on, you rich, spoilt brat.'

'So which car did we drive to Jaipur?' asked Bipin, after the first drink.

'I don't know …'

'You see what I mean?' Bipin pointed out.

It was time to start working on a consistent account of their short break to Jaipur.

29

THE POLICE

'WITH PHOTOGRAPHS OF THE TWO CRIMINALS IN THE local police's possession, we're all very confident that we'll make the arrests soon, sir,' Arfy updated his supervisor on the phone late that night.

'What makes you so confident?'

'Both Anuj Shastri and Bipin Desai are due back at work on Monday so it is a matter of days before they have to come out of their hidey-hole.'

'What if they don't? What if they've decided to leave their jobs? They're sitting on fifty-lakh rupees, if not more – I mean what do their jobs pay them anyway?'

'You have a point, sir,' Arfy appeased his supervisor, 'but Anuj's wife is expecting a child any minute; he has to come out even if he doesn't care about his low-paying job at the garage.'

'Hmm ... I hope you are correct, SI Khan – as you know, we are under a lot of pressure from the commissioner.'

'I understand, sir.'

'Keep an eye on his wife's place too.'

Like he hadn't thought about it already.

'We've deployed two men there too. Like I mentioned earlier, I'm quite confident that—'

The supervisor had already disconnected the line.

The police patrol was reduced for the night. The shops had closed so it was unnecessary to have all the plainclothes police officers on duty. With the crowd thinning, it would be conspicuous if there were too many men hanging around doing nothing. In any case, it was best if some of them went home and rested so they could return in the morning afresh and relieve those working through the night. The orders were clear. Upon spotting either or both of the suspects, they should inform the control tower instantly, and follow them. At no point should the suspects be out of sight of the officers who had spotted them. Bipin and Anuj were not to be approached until the backup teams arrived to take control. The last information they had on them from Rajendra was that at least one of them was armed. There was no need to put any lives at risk. A shootout in a public place, even at night, could end in a disaster.

Arfy left the police station around midnight, leaving instructions to be contacted at the earliest instance, if either of the two suspects was spotted.

30

FREE BIRDS

Thursday, 16 January 1997

7:30 a.m.

'I'VE ALREADY SPOKEN TO ONE BROKER,' BIPIN SAID, EVEN before they had got out of the bed.

'Spoken about what?'

'Hawala. If we want to transfer the money abroad to keep it in a foreign account for some time to be on the safe side.'

'But how long do we need to keep it there? And what if we need the money here, what then?'

'That's trickier. If we suddenly come into money, people will certainly notice. If questioned, how would we explain the source of funds?'

'Surely there must be some way, however roundabout. We can't just look at the cash and feel satisfied.'

'That's one way of enjoying it,' Bipin quipped. 'They say money has a lot of power, so maybe even looking at it might make us like Supermen?'

'On a serious note, what is the other way?'

'Other way?'

'You said one way of enjoying it is looking at it, so what's the other way of enjoying our hard-earned money?'

'We can start by conducting all our routine expenditure in cash and save our salaries month after month, but it will take years, probably decades to get to a crore.'

'Are you suggesting that despite all the money we have now, we live life exactly like the cockroaches we've always been?'

'What if we win a lottery?' The idea had just sprung into Bipin's mind.

'How do we do that?'

'It's rather simple actually. We find someone who wins the lottery of, say twenty lakhs, and we pay him twenty-two lakhs in cash and buy his ticket from him. Then, at least, we can explain to the tax authorities where the twenty-lakh rupees came from.'

'What about the rest – the ninety lakhs and then some?

'We'll worry about that later. To begin with, we'll have ample money to spend and move up in life a bit. We can gradually invest in shares or some small-time projects and tell people that we are earning decent returns. Nobody is going to question if we say we are earning more than we actually do. We'll pay taxes and turn it all into white money in a few years.'

'You are a genius.'

'Elementary, my dear Anuj, elementary.'

'Do you know what I want to do with the money?' Anuj asked.

'What?'

'I want to buy Munna ji's garage.'

'We can do that once we win the lottery,' Bipin passed a cheeky smile.

'I know, I know. I didn't mean I was going to buy it today or tomorrow.'

'What makes you think that Munna ji will want to sell his profitable business?'

'Everything is for sale, my friend, if the price is right.'

Both the friends closed their eyes, fantasizing about ways to spend and invest the money.

'I know we said Saturday or Sunday, but I think we could leave from here tomorrow after dark,' Bipin said after a while.

'I want to leave now; I want to see Manasi, I want to be with her.'

'I know, but we need to practise a little more patience now.'

'What about the Scotch you promised? I bet it is safe enough to go out and buy it now?'

'I remember my promise. I'll take a quick shower and go out. We also need milk, eggs and bread. What time is it?'

'Ten to eight,' Anuj replied. 'Will you go out alone?'

'Yes. If anyone is looking for us, we would be easier to spot together. Why give anyone a chance?'

'OK.'

'Promise me you won't leave the house until I come back.'

'Why would I do that? You'll be back in fifteen, twenty minutes, right?'

'If I get delayed for any reason, wait here for me. Please don't venture out and call Manasi or anyone.'

'In that case, how long should I wait for you to return?'

'Like you said, I shouldn't take more than twenty minutes. I'm only walking to the shops near Jai Cinema, so there's nothing to worry about. But in case something happens, like I get hit by a bus or get arrested—'

'Don't say such things, Bipin. They say if you think negatively, you bring ill luck upon yourself.'

'Nothing will happen, but listen to me carefully, please. Should something happen while I am out, do not leave this place until late Sunday evening under any circumstances. Stay put, okay my friend?'

'But what if you actually get arrested?'

'Then run, take as much cash as you can, and run.'

'How will I know if you're arrested?'

'It will surely be on the news. Keep watching.'

It had been his stupidity that got him apprehended; a real amateur mistake. But how could Bipin Desai have known the police had already identified him as one of the people involved in the heist? There had been no mention of it in the media. The local news had reported that the Noida Police was still looking for the two men – one old, one young. The reports said that the police were working on several lines of enquiry, which usually meant the police had nothing to go after. Nowhere was it mentioned that Gurgaon Police was also involved in the investigation and that they had identified the two suspects.

How did they know his name?

He had tried using his debit card to withdraw some cash since he was the one preaching to Anuj that they shouldn't spend the cash from the heist to buy the Scotch and other supplies. What had he been thinking when he had put that damn card in the machine? And when the machine had swallowed his card, why hadn't he simply walked away? It had not occurred to him that the police might have called the bank to block his cards. He had assumed something was wrong with the machine, and walked into the nearest shop and to call and inform the bank about the faulty machine.

As he dialled the bank's number and listened to the boring elevator hold-music, four plainclothes police officers were on him like a rash.

31

JAILBIRDS

SO, WHERE IS THE CASH, SONNY BOY?' ARFY ASKED.

'In Gurgaon.'

'I know that, sonny boy. We know both you and Ajay were—'

'Anuj Shastri.'

'Fine. We know you and *Anuj* Shastri went underground somewhere in Gurgaon, but where? I want the address to recover the stolen cash.'

'It is near the Old Railway Road between sectors four and five.'

'House number?'

'A 1065.'

'Thank you.'

'When can I meet Anuj?' Bipin thought it was best to meet his friend and explain personally rather than let the crooked inspector manipulate him by saying that Bipin had squealed.

'In a minute. I'll just give this address to my team, and then you and your friend can have a hug. Tonight you can even share the cell, okay?'

Bipin nodded. He could feel his eyes moistening.

'Mr Sharma, do you want to come out or stay with your client while we wait for the stolen money to be retrieved?'

'Thank you, SI Khan, but I'd like to stay with my client.'

'Sure.' Arfy walked out.

Bipin and Sharma heard the door lock.

'Why have they locked *me* inside?' Sharma looked perturbed. This hadn't happened before.

———

The door opened after two hours and Arfy walked in smoothly. 'All good,' he said. 'My team has picked up the cash, sonny boy.'

'SI Khan, I hope you won't forget your promise.'

'What promise?'

'You promised that my client will get half the prison time.'

'Are you a real advocate, Mr Sharma?'

'What do you mean?'

'I don't remember making any promise to you or anyone.' Arfy said sternly.

'But you said—'

'Where's the proof? Did I sign any papers?'

'But you made a promise!'

'To whom?'

'To us, to Bipin and me.'

'I don't remember.'

'How could you not remember? This is unethical.'

'Well, I don't. You can't decide what I remember or I don't, can you?' Arfy pointed towards the red recording light that was currently off. 'Remember, you had asked me to switch off the recording? In court, it's your word against mine. By tomorrow morning, sonny boy here will be a convicted felon, so his word won't count.'

'You cannot do this.'

'I'll see what I can do, no promises.' Arfy passed a wicked smile, then ignoring Advocate Sharma's agape mouth, he opened the door and called out, 'Bhim Singh, please take sonny boy to the cell.'

Bugger!

Bhim Singh, looking dour as expected, walked in and handcuffed Bipin, who didn't know how to react. Had the comedian fooled them into believing they had a deal when they had nothing? Had he given away the address for nothing? And honestly, was Sharma a real advocate? How had the idiot missed ensuring proper paperwork for their deal?

If he could, Bipin would have turned around and punched Sharma in the face, but his hands were cuffed behind his back now.

As he walked out, he finally saw Anuj. He was handcuffed too. Another police constable was holding him.

Bipin felt cheated, but he thought it served him right. He had succumbed to a deal condemning his friend to serve twice the prison time as him. It was only right to acknowledge his wrong behaviour and apologize.

'I'm sorry,' he uttered softly when he got close to Anuj.

'Why did you tell them?'

'I had no choice. If I hadn't told Arfy, you would have—' Bipin tried to explain to his friend.

'Arfy? Who's *Arfy*?'

'Senior Inspector Arfy Khan.'

'Who is that?'

'The joker who has been playing us against each other since yesterday.'

'Playing who, playing what, Bipin? Are you okay? What are you talking about? Did they drug you or something?'

'Stop feigning ignorance; I know you were ready to take the deal.'

'Which deal? You left me at the Gurgaon house yesterday morning to pick up milk, eggs and booze. I waited for you all day yesterday and today, until the police came into the house to arrest me because you gave them the address, you idiot.'

'So you mean you weren't ...'

The penny finally dropped for Bipin. And it descended rather profoundly.

Anuj or Amit or Anup or Arup Shastri was not being questioned in the other room ... Anuj had not hired any female lawyer, diabetic or otherwise ... he didn't have any lawyer, because he had not even been arrested. Senior Inspector Arfy Khan wasn't as absent-minded as he had purported to Bipin ... he wasn't clumsy or foolish at all ... the falling and tripping were all a huge stunt? Arfy had manipulated Bhola and Birju and Babul and Badal Desai into providing him with the information where the cash was ... also where Anuj was ... all the stories and fables and analogies, they were all shenanigans. Arfy had blinded him with fake punches and made him reveal ... everything without offering anything in return. Anuj, Alok, Atul and Arup were all four-letter names starting with the letter A. If Arfy was so forgetful, how come he always came up with a name that so closely resembled Anuj's actual name? Arfy would have had to remember the real name to come up with a close-fitting new one, wouldn't he? But what was the point of retrospection? He should have grasped it back then, caught out the inspector's lies; it was far too late in the day now ... their dream over, their gilded world ripped asunder.

That bastard!

From the corner of his eye he saw Senior Inspector Arfy Khan wave at him from a distance. 'Want another Thums Up, sonny boy?' he shouted, flashed a wicked smile, then turned and said something softly to Bhim Singh, who started walking towards them.

THE TRUTH BEHIND THE STORY

A PORTION OF THIS STORY IS BASED ON TRUE EVENTS, EVEN though I've modified, extrapolated and fictionalized them for this novel.

A close friend of mine, Roma – I can't mention her real name for reasons I shall explain in a bit – worked for a large retail chain, back in the nineties. The company was listed on the Bombay Stock Exchange, but the majority shares and hence, the control, were held by an influential family. Most of the transactions were in cash which the stores secured in a safe for a few days before a van came to pick it up twice a week.

The facts:

- The cash travelled in exactly the same fashion as described in the book.
- The driver was unarmed; the whole operation was successful only because no one except a handful of employees knew about it.

- The accountants declared the turnover as dictated by their employers, since it translated into profits, which translated into tax. All in all, it was an exercise in tax evasion.

The fiction:

- The name of the company. To the best of my knowledge, there is no retail brand called RealStores.
- The actual business wasn't related to supermarkets.
- I've tweaked the number of stores and their turnovers. It is to be noted that one crore in 1997 is approximately thirty-five crores today.
- I've changed the location of the business. I picked Noida so that even the location of the retail chain remains undisclosed.
- The daylight robbery, obviously, never took place.

The reason I cannot disclose Roma's real name is that it could give away her identity. In the digitally connected world of today, one search on LinkedIn by any of you would reveal the names of the past companies she has worked for, and some of you would easily be able to work out the name of the actual retail company where this practice of tax evasion was commonplace. Roma was kind enough to share the little secret with me privately, and I don't intend to get her into legal trouble. Also, I have no intentions of being pulled into a lengthy court case myself, which the company, if identified, might file.

I know for a fact that the said chain of retail stores does not exist anymore.

In any event, the heart of this story isn't where and why the cash was being transported or how much; it's about the heist and the intriguing phenomenon known as prisoner's dilemma. I hope you liked it.